FAINTLEY SPEAKING

If an impecunious author had not accidentally intercepted a telephone call, the mysterious Miss Faintley might have defied even Mrs Bradley's efforts at solution, The telephone message began, 'Faintley speaking . . .' and proceeded with instructions to collect a parcel from the local railway station and deliver it to a somewhat shady shopkeeper. The author not only delivered the parcel but also unwisely demanded payment for doing so . . .

Not long after, Miss Faintley was murdered. It seemed at first unlikely that she, a prim, quiet schoolmistress, could have anthing to do with crime. Yet Mrs Bradley's investigations led to some exciting developments . . .

FAINTLEY
SPEAKING

Gladys Mitchell

BC MC

First published 1954
by
Michael Joseph

This edition 2001 by Chivers Press
published by arrangement with
the author's estate

ISBN 0 7540 8596 1

British Library Cataloguing in Publication Data available

Printed and bound in Great Britain by
Bookcraft, Midsomer Norton, Somerset

To

Ella Vinall & Barbara Blattler,
their cat, their caravan
and all

CONTENTS

CHAPTER ONE

MANDSELL

*

'I prythee, gentle mortal, speak again.'
SHAKESPEARE – *A Midsummer Night's Dream*

'I'M sure I'm very sorry, Mr Mandsell,' said his landlady, 'but I've come to the finish. I been kept waiting six weeks for my money, and I'd have you to realize, sir, as I can't be kept waiting for ever. I've got to live, sir, and so has Deaks, same like as what you have, sir.'

'Why should any of us worry about living, Mrs Deaks? Life's not so hot. On the other hand, think how it enriches your character, if not exactly your pocket, to provide the indigent like me with two meals a day and a bed! Just think, too, of the good you're doing yourself with the Recording Angel.'

'It's no use, sir. Sorry as I am to lose you . . . for I'm sure you've been no trouble and have always spoke gentlemanly and took your hat off to me in the street as there's them that wouldn't . . . this is my last word. Twice have I let you stop on as you have talked me into it, but never no more. Supper and bed and breakfast you've had these six weeks gone, and what have I got to show for it? No, sir, sorry as I am, as I can't say more, and much as I've liked your company, it has got to be O.U.T. unless you can pay me by Saturday.'

'But, look here, Mrs Deaks, you know you'll be paid as soon as I get my advance! I've told you I must wait for publication. You *know* my novel's been accepted. I showed you the letter. The money's *there* all right!'

'Be that as it may, sir, even if *I* was willing to wait, well, Deaks, he isn't, and that's the flat of it, if you take my meaning plain. Pay up or go ... them's his words and I can't go again 'em and don't intend to.'

'All right, Mrs Deaks, that's fair enough. I don't intend to land you in trouble with your husband. But Deaks needn't worry, you know. I shall pay you as soon as I'm able to, and when my ship comes home you'll look pretty silly at the thought that you chucked me out, especially on a filthy night like this.'

'Oh,' exclaimed the landlady, turning her head as a torrent of summer rain hurtled spitefully at the window, 'I never meant you'd got to get out *to-night*, sir! I wouldn't be hard like that, and nor would Deaks.'

'Nevertheless, I'm going. I suppose I'd better get myself pinched in order to have somewhere to sleep.' His light tone was gone. He was extremely sensitive, and spoke bitterly.

'You wouldn't do that, sir? Not really?' She was distressed – a middle-aged, decent, kindly soul.

'Wouldn't I? Of course I shall go. You'll have to let me leave my books and things here for a day or two until I get fixed up somewhere else.' He wondered where the somewhere else could be. He had no one from whom to borrow.

Receiving her tearful consent, he went upstairs, put on his raincoat and hat, refilled his fountain-pen and walked out of the house. In his pockets he had a small notebook, a sixpence, fivepence-halfpenny, his pen, a pencil, a penknife, his mother's wedding-ring, and his publisher's contract calling for two more novels. He supposed he would have to get a job. It was a pity when he had the plot of the next novel so clearly in his head, but it could not be helped.

He walked rapidly in the direction of the Public Library with the intention of consulting the advertisement columns of the newspapers while the library doors were still open. At least he would be under cover. But he had overlooked the fact that it was Thursday. All departments of the library were shut. He stood in the rain and cursed himself. He could have stayed in his lodgings until the morning, or even until Saturday. There had been no suggestion of turning him out at a moment's notice, and it was teeming down cats and dogs. Well, he was not going back to beg for shelter when it was his own tom-fool pride that had brought him out on such an evening.

Thoroughly angry, and already extremely wet, he put his hands in his raincoat pocket, lowered his head and walked towards the High Street. He had eaten nothing since break-fast. (The arrangement was that he always got his lunch out.) In the High Street there would be presented to him the alternatives of punching a policeman or spending one or two pence on bread. Then he remembered that it was Thursday. None of the shops would be open. It would have to be the policeman, he concluded. There was always one on point duty. No, of course there was not! . . . never on Thursdays or Sundays, because the shops were shut and then traffic was almost non-existent in the little provincial town and no point duty was needed.

The rain still poured down. The shop blinds, usually let down all day in summer to protect the goods from the sun, had been taken in, so that their shelter was lost. Mandsell became wet through, and was thoroughly wretched. Already he was beginning to change his mind. After all, there was nothing for it, he felt, but to go back to his lodgings for the night. Mrs Deaks would feel relieved, he knew, and even the unwelcoming Deaks could scarcely refuse to take him in. He must pocket his pride and go and ask, anyhow. It was hopeless to think of staying out all night in weather like this! His chest had always been troublesome.

He turned and began to walk back. As there was now no point in returning by way of the Public Library he took a road which ran alongside the park. Half-way up there was a public telephone box. At the sight of it he had an inspira-tion. His publisher's office was on the telephone. There would be no harm in making a note of the number, if only to get out of the pelting rain for a minute or two. On the morrow he would telephone to ask whether there was any prospect of obtaining a small percentage of his advance royalties. It was not exactly asking for charity. The book was up there; it had been accepted for publication. If he could get the publisher to advance him the six weeks' rent he owed, Mrs Deaks would look after him for another few weeks on tick again while he looked for a job. He could not imagine why this excellent idea had not occurred to him before.

Feeling suddenly elated and hopeful, he strode towards the telephone box. Just before he reached it, a man, with his collar turned up to his ears and his hat pulled down against the rain, came out of the box and walked rapidly away from Mandsell down the otherwise deserted road.

'Must have needed to phone pretty urgently to come out in weather like this,' thought Mandsell, pulling open the door and entering the box. Just as the door closed behind him the telephone began to buzz. Acting on instinct he picked up the receiver and said, 'Hallo?'

'Oh, there you are! I'm sorry to be so late, but the last one has only just gone out!' It was a woman's voice he heard.

'I think there's some mistake,' he began.

'No, there isn't. This is Faintley speaking.'

'It isn't faint. It's quite clear. But, you see – '

'Miss Faintley, idiot! Don't waste time making stupid jokes. Somebody may come in again at any minute, and you know what they are for minding other people's business! Why, it would be all over the place in no time if one of them overheard me! Now, you *do* understand, don't you?'

'Not a thing. You see – '

'Oh, no, do listen, please. You said you'd help me, and I've nobody else I can trust. The parcel is at Hagford Station, and all you've got to do is to ask for it in my name, and take it along to Tomson. Don't forget to ask for a receipt. It's awfully good of you. I don't know what I should have done if . . . Oh, dear! Good-bye. I can hear them in the vestibule. It was an awfully good idea to ring you up on a public phone. Much better than settling things here, with all these busybodies about!'

'What number are you speaking from?' he demanded; but there was no reply.

Mandsell hung up. What a silly woman! Surely she could hear the difference between his voice and that of the man she had arranged to ring up! He opened the telephone directory, found the number he wanted, copied it into his notebook – fortunately the electric light in the little box was functioning! – and went out again into the rain. The more he thought about the telephone conversation . . . if conversation was the word for it . . . *he* had not been able to get a word in edgeways! . . . the more it intrigued him. He was inclined, in fact, to execute the commission he had been given. Hagford was the next station up the line, a five-mile walk. It would be something definite to do, and that was always fun. He found that he was grateful for the small adventure, and, in any case, all was grist that came to an author's mill. With a bit of luck, the incident might make a short story for the evening paper, now that he came to think of it.

Tomson? Mandsell was certain he had seen the name up somewhere. A shop, of course. Oh, yes, one of a mean little terrace of shops in Fish Street. Tomson's was the one in the middle, a small, dingy, drapery establishment. Mandsell had often wondered how such places even made enough to pay the rent, let alone feed and clothe the proprietor. It was said that such shops usually had a second string to their bow, and that, behind the giant red herring of their ostensible business, all kinds of semi-legal and sometimes downright criminal practices were carried on . . . thieves' kitchens, abortions, proscribed forms of gambling, brothels, shady little night-clubs, black-market deals, and white-slave exchanges went through Mandsell's imaginative mind . . . and that the police were powerless to interfere without such definite evidence as it was almost impossible to procure.

What Tomson's particular racket might be there was no means of guessing by merely looking at the jaded collection of cheap underclothes and second-hand shoes in the window, but, armed with the parcel and with the name of Miss Faintley to conjure with, there might be a chance of obtaining a peep behind the scenes. Mandsell began to see himself as the writer of a scandalous but highly successful novel of low life, one that was banned in Spain and Eire, preached against in the Welsh chapels and smuggled out of sight of their teen-age children by people who would have been horrified to find it in a public library.

Sunk in this blissful dream of best-selling authorship, it did not take him long to reach his lodgings. He no longer felt like a wet stray dog seeking a home. For one thing, he felt certain that his publisher would advance him that small, convenient loan . . . after all, the book was *there* – it was accepted! . . . and for another he was now in a position to inform Deaks that a woman had given him a job. It would be unnecessary to explain that it was an unpaid one! Besides, it would not be unpaid in the long run if he got a short story and possibly a best-seller of a novel out of it.

Considerably cheered, he beat on the front door of the quiet little house and his landlord opened it. He grunted when he saw who it was, but did not hesitate to let Mandsell in. He was not a hard-hearted man; besides, he had had to listen for the past hour to his wife's accusations of having driven that poor young fellow away in weather which was not fit for a dog, let alone a gentleman as had been to Oxford College.

He pointed with the stem of his pipe.

'Better go straight through and take off them sopping wet clo'es in the scullery, sir, else Mother 'ull be on my tail again. There's my overcoat behind the kitchen door. Take it in as you go. It'll do to slip on while you has a warm at the kitchen fire.'

Next day Mandsell spent the morning working out his short story, and in the afternoon set off to collect Miss Faintley's parcel. He felt and looked a very different young man from the soaked and despairing adventurer who had gone into the telephone box on the previous night. Nothing more had been said about his leaving his lodgings; his trousers had been dried and nicely pressed, his shoes cleaned and his socks laundered, and Mrs Deaks had even salved her conscience by giving him lunch – cod with parsley sauce and new potatoes.

He walked jauntily. The afternoon was bright and pleasant without being hot, and, once he was clear of Kindleford, the walk was invitingly rural, the flattish country intersected by streams, the great trees shady, the fields filled with buttercups or poppies and corn, the hedges still bearing wild roses and here and there the first flowers of Traveller's Joy.

All too soon came the dingy outskirts of Hagford, at no time a prepossessing town, and, after the open country, of unspeakable dreariness. A long stretch of council houses, not even relieved by shops, led at last to the centre of the town and to the railway station. Before he went on to collect the parcel, Mandsell saw a post office and decided to telephone his publisher from there, but he realized, before he lifted the receiver, that he had not sufficient money for the trunk call which would be necessary, and he felt he could scarcely ask for the charges to be reversed!

He came out to the counter, asked for a letter-card, wrote it (thankful that he had his own pen on him, and so had no need to use the abominable instrument provided by the Government), posted it, and reviewed his diminished assets. The sooner his publisher answered, the better, he thought grimly.

He soon found the station, went to the Left Luggage office and asked for a parcel addressed to Miss Faintley. He thought that the clerk gave him a sharp glance, but he did not ask for any evidence that Mandsell had the righ* to collect the parcel. He handed over a flat package neatly secured with sealing-wax and string, remarked that it was a nice day, and retired to an inside office.

Mandsell turned the parcel over once or twice and read the superscription:

Miss L. Faintley, B.Sc.
Kindleford School
Kindleford

He tried to guess what was underneath the brown paper, sealing-wax, and string. Except that it might be something made of wood he could gain no clue to the contents. He was glad to be out of Hagford and in the open country again, but he wanted his tea and hoped that Mrs Deaks would still be in her generous mood of the morning.

He found Tomson's shop, which was exactly where he had believed it would be, walked in, and handed the parcel over the counter. He had walked some little distance down the street when he remembered that he had not asked for a receipt. He went back and rapped on the counter.

'Sorry to trouble you,' he remarked to the seedy little man who had taken the parcel from him, 'but I forgot to ask for a receipt.'

'Receipt for what, sir?'

'Miss Faintley's parcel, of course.'

'Parcel, sir?'

'Oh, come on, now, buck up! I brought in a smallish flat parcel about three minutes ago. I should have asked for a receipt, but I forgot.'

'I'm sorry, but you're mistaken. I've not taken in no parcels for no one.'

'What? Oh, but, look here – '

'You've made a mistake. This is a drapery business, not Pickford's. I don't take in parcels for nobody, and I never took no parcels for you. And my foot is on the burglar alarm if so be you thought of coming it funny.' His tone was both frightened and menacing.

'Look,' said Mandsell. 'I'm not thinking of coming it funny. That is beyond my scope. Do you seriously stand there and deny that I handed in to you a small flat parcel in the name of Miss Faintley, and that you accepted it without any query?'

'I seriously think you're suffering from sunstroke, young feller. You go home and have a quiet lay down.'

This advice infuriated Mandsell.

'This is Tomson's, isn't it?' he demanded.

'At your service, sir. And now,' said the proprietor

savagely, 'get out, or I'll call a policeman. I know your sort!'

At this, a berserk rage overcame Mandsell. Like most young men, the thing he detested chiefly was the thought that someone was trying to make a fool of him. He leaned over the counter and gripped the small proprietor by the tie. He drew him towards the counter until the little man's head was half-way over a pile of fancy scarves stacked almost under Mandsell's nose.

'Come off it!' the young man said fiercely. 'Don't you dare try to pull this stunt on me! I don't know what was in the parcel, but I'm jolly sure – '

At this moment the shop-bell rang and in walked two middle-aged women. Mandsell, with a last despairing tug at the proprietor's tie, turned and walked out. He walked fast. As he walked, three thoughts were in his mind. One was that there was something mysterious, not to say fishy, about the parcel; the second was that he was unlikely to get any reply, favourable or otherwise, from his publisher until Tuesday morning at the earliest; the third was that his publisher's telephone number had always been on the letter of acceptance which he had received when he sent in his book.

He began to slacken his pace. Then a desperate idea came to him. He went back to the shop. It was empty. The two customers had gone, and the proprietor was not to be seen. Mandsell rapped imperatively on the counter and the man came shuffling out. He looked surprised and alarmed when he saw the young man, but, recovering quickly, said:

'You hop it, or I'll call the police!'

'I've already done that. Parcel or receipt, please. They'll be here directly.'

'Nothing doing. You're mistaken. I haven't got no parcel of yourn. I may have a parcel for a lady named Faintley, but that ain't nothing to do with you.' The man's tone had altered. Mandsell felt victorious.

'All right. There's the clerk at Hagford Station who handed me the parcel, you know. I've got a witness.'

'What'll you take to forget him?'

'Take? I'll take a receipt.'

'Oh, come, now, mister! I'm not putting my name to nothing. What will you take? That's what I ask you. Five quid any good?'

'Since you ask me . . . yes.' (It would satisfy Mrs Deaks for the moment.) The man opened the till. He took out four one-pound and two ten-shilling notes and thrust them across the counter.

'Get out of here!' he said thickly. 'And, remember, that's blackmail money, that is! I've got you *where* I want you *when* I want you if you pick up them notes. What about it?'

Mandsell picked up the notes.

'There's one thing . . . *you* can hardly demand a receipt,' he said, as he put them into an inside pocket. 'Thanks a lot. I'll repay you when my ship comes home. I regard this as temporary accommodation only. Meanwhile I must admit that it comes in handy. So long. I'll be seeing you! The police won't – *this* time!'

He went straight back to his lodgings and gave Mrs Deaks four pounds, the result of a bluff which had worked.

'Well, I *must* say, sir!' she observed, immensely surprised.

'I know it isn't much,' said Mandsell, 'but if you wouldn't mind trusting me a bit longer . . . ' He was immensely pleased with himself, the man of action, and went up to his room to complete and polish the short story for which his recent experiences had given him the idea. He intended to spend the whole evening on the job. Mrs Deaks was bringing him tea and supper. But between him and his work came niggling, unanswerable questions.

What was in the parcel, that the man Tomson had been prepared to pay him five pounds blackmail money? (For blackmail, surely, was what it must amount to, as the shopkeeper himself had pointed out.)

Why could not the woman who called herself Miss Faintley have accomplished her own errand?

Who was the man who should have been her correspondent and who had walked out of the telephone booth just before she rang him up, and why had this man not waited any longer? Ringing people up on a public telephone was always a chancy sort of business. Of course, they had chosen a box which was not likely to be used much during the evening, but the woman could have had no guarantee that somebody else would not have been in the box at the time she had arranged to speak.

If the parcel was required so urgently at Tomson's it must be important. If so, why had she been in such a hurry to give her instructions that she had not even troubled to verify whether or not she was talking to the right man? Was she in desperate straits about the parcel? (That seemed likely, judging by the shopkeeper's reactions.) Was she also unaccustomed to talking on the telephone, so that all voices (particularly men's voices) were exactly alike to her?

Answer came there none, and Mandsell, secure in his lodgings for another week or two, shrugged, and continued with his work. Nevertheless, his mind was far from easy. The five pounds were all very well . . . in fact, undeniably useful . . . but what, he wondered, did the acceptance of them entail? Had he become an accessory to crime? Did the parcel contain pornographic postcards or 'curious' literature? Did it contain atomic secrets, or even a new kind of time-bomb which could not be safely left at the station beyond a certain limit of hours?

Suppose he had helped to bring nearer the spectre of another world war! Suppose he had assisted to blow up the Prime Minister or Miss Gracie Fields!

Well, the matter was out of his hands. If any of these things happened, he hoped he would never know. He took out his remaining pound, turned it over, and then went out and bought himself a drink.

CHAPTER TWO

MARK

*

'The way of an eagle in the air; the way of a serpent upon a rock; the way of a ship in the midst of the sea.'

Proverbs XXX. 19

MARK was angry with his parents. At thirteen he considered himself old enough to tour France on his bicycle with his friend Ellison. That his parents . . . his mother in particular . . . should condemn him instead to a fortnight at the seaside village of Cromlech seemed the height of unreasoning injustice. That Ellison's parents had been equally obstructive served only as a mild palliative, and, anyway, Ellison was not staying in Cromlech, so that Cromlech was quite intolerable.

Mark brooded, kicking a stone in front of him down the rough path which led from the panoramic cliff-top to the beach. Two further insults smouldered in his breast. Not only was a teacher from his school staying at his hotel, but, through the treachery of Mark's father, Mark had been compelled to accept an invitation from this loathsome interloper to visit the cathedral town of Torbury, a complete waste of a whole fine day. What was worst of all, the wretched teacher was a *woman*!

'Hope her beastly breakfast chokes her!' thought Mark, referring to his teacher. 'Silly clot!' He swung his towel moodily at a clump of sea-pinks. 'My last bathe for twenty-four hours, I expect! Hope I get cramp and drown! That'll show them!'

His thoughts continued along an already well-worn track. If only it had been a *decent master* . . . Mr Taylor, perhaps, or Mr Roberts . . . he would not have minded so much; but

of course it *would* have to be old Semi-Conscious! *Faintley*!
What a name! Fancy anybody with a name like that not
changing it! Of all the cissy-sounding names ever inherited
by human beings, Faintley seemed to Mark, during these
embittered hours, the most ridiculous and undesirable.

The path wound right and left in its serpentine progress
down the cliff. Sometimes it broke into a cascade of
broad, uneven steps, and occasionally, at a bend, there was
a seat and a view of the coast. Mark, intent on his wrongs,
and also on his swim, ignored these amenities and flopped
his rubber-shod feet uncompromisingly downhill.

Trees and shrubs grew thickly; ferns appeared in modest,
dim, damp places; over the bay the gulls swooped, hovered
and cried. There was a very faint mist on the sea. In spite
of himself, Mark began to feel better. He glanced at his
wrist-watch, a present for a respectable end-of-the-year
report (although even *that* old Semi-Conscious had tried to
muck up with her usual bit of sarcasm and a C where Mark
would have awarded himself a B minus). He noted that the
time was half-past six. Breakfast at the hotel was not until
nine. He would swim for about twenty minutes . . . it was
too cold to stay in long in the early morning . . . and then
when he was dressed he would walk along the sands to the
far arm of the bay. He had spotted a path which led over
the further headland. It might be a private path. He jolly
well hoped it was . . . a spot of trespassing would just about
fit his mood.

But his mood was altering rapidly. It occurred to him
that he and Ellison had brought to perfection . . . or near it;
you could not pull it off with Snotty Joe, the senior assistant . . . the art of *losing* the teachers-in-charge on school
outings. It would be rather a rag to lose Faintley, and have
a day out by himself. He had plenty of money. He had
been saving it secretly for weeks in the hope of making
that cherished trip to France.

He decided he would show his father and Miss Faintley
that you could take a horse to Torbury but you could not
get it into the Cathedral if it did not want to go!

Almost happy at last, Mark took the last flight of steps with a leap and a stumble, and began to plough through dry sand. He pulled off his sweater and shorts, remembered to unstrap his wrist-watch, kicked off his shoes. The fresh air played round his bare shoulders. Gosh . . . it was cold! He had better get in quick! The tide was making, so that was all right, thank goodness. It was not a good thing in those waters to swim on an outgoing tide. Mark summoned his resolution . . . his thin body was sensitive to cold . . . took a breath and dashed boldly forward and into the icy, green sea.

He had been swimming for about twenty minutes and was lazily floating on his back when an addition to his first plan occurred to him. Suppose he could contrive, somehow or other, to make old Semi-Conscious look a fool! He realized that the close co-operation of one's form-mates was usually necessary to ensure the success of such an enterprise, nevertheless he toyed with the idea and had arrived at the unchivalrous stage of visualizing Miss Faintley, in the hands of two large vergers, being frog-marched in ignominy from the Cathedral when, turning over with the intention of taking a final quick swim before making for the shore, he became aware that his privacy had been invaded by a young woman. Mark was in no mood for this. He despised the whole sex, and had no intention of sharing the sea with an Amazonian girl, particularly with one who obviously could give him forty yards in a hundred and still beat him.

He dog-paddled into shallow water and waded out, but the young woman swam towards him and called out cheerfully:

'Hullo! How did you find it?'

'Cold,' said Mark.

'Oh, I don't know. It doesn't seem bad to me.' She turned from him, ducked into a wave and went out to sea like a torpedo. Mark watched in envious admiration; then, afraid that she might turn, and, seeing him watching, imagine that he admired her prowess, he picked up his towel and began to rub his hair. He was dry and dressed in a very few minutes, but by the time he had tramped along the sand to the opposite side of the bay (it was much farther off than he had supposed) the tide was so high that it was impossible to get round the bend and climb up the headland path.

He turned and walked back along the beach. The girl was still in the sea. Mark, in spite of a strong natural aversion to females, had the instincts of a sportsman. He stood at the edge and waved. The girl caught sight of him and came swimming in.

'I say,' shouted Mark, 'it isn't safe to stay in much longer. The tide's nearly turning, I think.'

'Thanks for telling me. Where are you staying?'

'The *Whitesand*.'

'Good. So are we.'

'I haven't seen you there.'

'Came late last night in my cabin cruiser and turned up at the *Whitesand* at two a.m. Had to knock them up. They weren't pleased. Well, see you later on, I expect.'

She made for the shore. Mark shuffled away through loose sand, sat down on the first set of steps, shook surplus sand out of his shoes and tramped stolidly skywards towards breakfast. Her cabin cruiser! It only needed that! And *he* had to go to Torbury Cathedral with the Faintley!

The beginning of the excursion with Miss Faintley was fully as futile and exasperating as Mark had known it would be. To begin with, although the bus ride took fully an hour and three-quarters, Miss Faintley refused to travel on top.

'No, Street,' she said, 'I dislike the smell of stale tobacco smoke.' And, to Mark's intense annoyance, she even gave him a slight but unmistakable push to ensure that he really did go inside the bus.

'All right. You wait,' thought Mark. He insisted upon taking the gangway seat and upon paying Miss Faintley's fare as well as his own. He was so ruffled that he contemplated paying full fare for himself by way of asserting his independence, but reconsidered this rash plan and paid a half-fare as usual. During the journey Miss Faintley chatted unceasingly. Mark gave her half his attention. The other half was busy with plans of escaping as soon as he possibly could. It ought to be fairly easy. Torbury was a big place. There would be bookshops on the way to the Cathedral. The Faintley would be certain to want to look at books. She always did, even on school outings; yes, even on the one to the Science Museum, Mark reminded himself.

'Excuse me, but I want to buy a film for my camera,' he said, when at last they got off the bus and were passing a chemist's shop.

'Very well, Street. I'll be looking in the window next door. There seem to be some interesting books.' Miss Faintley seemed pleased, Mark thought.

There were several people in the chemist's shop. Mark waited to be served, and, whilst he was waiting, he saw that his way of escape was assured. The shop had a second entrance from a street at the back. He obtained his film and left by this further door. Out in the street, he turned and hurried back towards the bus station. A bus was just moving off. He leapt on board, climbed to the top and discovered that the bus was turning into the very street in which he had abandoned his teacher. He looked out of the window, but there was no sign of Miss Faintley.

'Gone in to browse and forgotten all about me, the silly ass,' thought Mark.

'Where do you want, sonny?' inquired the conductor. Mark replied (with a vague recollection of the map which Miss Faintley had insisted upon showing him):

'The river. Do you go there?'

The conductor said, 'Twopenny half,' and clipped him a ticket. Mark got off at the bridge, stood himself a stodge at a café . . . fish and chips, apple pie and ice cream . . . and then went for a two-shilling steamer trip. He spent a thoroughly satisfactory day, had tea at the same café upon his return, and had prepared a convincing, innocent-sounding story for his parents by the time he got back to the hotel. There was only one snag. He had no idea of what Miss Faintley's story would be. His parents, however, were out when he arrived, so he bathed and changed and went down to the lounge, hoping to find Miss Faintley and try out on her the rather reproachful remarks he had concocted.

'I'd no *idea* where you'd got to,' he would say, 'so after I'd looked for you ... not knowing Torbury and it being such a whacking big place ... where *did* you get to, Miss Faintley? I mean, I know I must have kept you waiting a jolly long time while I bought my film, but the shop was simply packed with people, and once I'd gone in I didn't much like to walk out again without buying anything ... they might think I'd shop-lifted something ...'

By this time Miss Faintley would have interrupted to give *her* version, Mark hoped, and the rest of the conversation would follow accordingly. Unfortunately, Miss Faintley was not in the lounge, and the story, as told to Mark's parents at dinner, did not seem nearly as convincing as Mark had hoped. However, Mark's father (with who knows what personal recollections of boyhood!) stemmed the tide of his wife's remonstrances.

'It's all right, Margaret. Nothing's happened. The only thing is ... where has Miss Faintley got to? She certainly isn't in here, and dinner goes off at nine.'

Miss Faintley was not at breakfast, either. Mark did not go for an early swim; it was raining. He met the girl who had spoken to him the morning before, and found that she was accompanied by a quietly-discomforting old woman as yellow as the gamboge in Mark's paint-box and as extravagantly dressed as a macaw. The younger woman came up to him after breakfast.

'The rain's stopped. I'm going in. Coming?'

Mark thought he might as well. He said as much, and went upstairs to get his things. When he came back into the hotel vestibule the manager was there, talking to his father. Both turned to Mark. 'What about this Miss Faintley who took you out yesterday? You know she hasn't come back to the hotel,' the manager said. Mark said he was sorry. He did know, but had no helpful observations to offer.

'I suppose you mean she hasn't paid,' he said. 'She's a teacher at our school, so I suppose she'll pay all right, in the end, you know.'

'I hope so, but that isn't what's worrying us, sonny. I've rung the hospital and the police station at Torbury. Neither knows anything about her.'

'Any reason to suppose there's any funny business?' asked Mark's father.

'No, but one has to inquire when guests don't come back at night. Have you known the lady long, Mr Street, may I ask?'

'I forgot when she first came,' Mark replied at a glance from his father. 'Nobody at school likes her much,' he added, 'but you don't seem to think of her doing anything *queer*. Of course, she might have got drowned,' he added helpfully. At this moment his acquaintance of the previous morning, her handsome frame draped in slacks and a Sloppy Joe, came to the foot of the stairs. She carried a waterproof bag. Thankfully Mark gathered up his own belongings and followed the girl to the swing-door. In less than ten minutes they were both in the water.

'What's the trouble?' the girl asked, as both of them surfaced. 'The manager looked a bit jaundiced, I thought . . . or is that my imagination?'

Mark explained, quite truthfully, exactly what had happened on the previous day.

'Of course, if I'd known, I wouldn't have left her,' Mark concluded.

'Why not? You couldn't have known she would drop out like that. Where do you suppose she's got to?'

'I don't know. I keep wondering. She's an awful ass, but . . . well, I mean, it isn't the *asses* who disappear usually, is it? It's people who are making a getaway. I'm sure Miss Faintley isn't one of those. She wouldn't have pluck enough, for one thing. I say, what's your name?'

'Laura Menzies. I know yours. I saw it in the visitors' book when we arrived. You're Mark Street, aren't you? I'll call you Mark and you'd better call me Laura.'

'All right,' agreed Mark. 'Race you to the diving-raft!'

He gave himself a generous lead by setting off as the words left his mouth, but Laura Menzies beat him easily and had hoisted herself on to the raft by the time he had threshed his way to it and was holding on to the side.

'Not bad,' she said casually. 'I expect you do most of your swimming in a public bath, don't you?'

Mark admitted that he did, and clambered out to sit beside her.

'I say,' he said, 'old Faintley, you know. What do you *honestly* think? I mean, if she'd been run over she'd have been taken to hospital, and what was funniest . . . only I haven't told anybody yet . . . you know that bookshop she went to when I left her to buy my film? Well, she wasn't there any more. I mean, she wasn't inside, either, because I could see in from the top of the bus. At the time I thought what a bit of luck, but now I'm beginning to wonder whether she might have thought it wasn't a bad idea to push off by herself after all.'

'There's something in that.'

'I think so, too. After all, why did she want to take me out in the first place? It wasn't as though I'd got nothing else to do. You don't suppose . . . ' he hitched himself round to look at her instead of continuing to watch his own feet gently scuffling in the sea . . . 'you don't suppose she was using me for some kind of cover? I've read of things like that. Do you think she could have got mixed up with some sort of gang, and took me with her to put them off the scent?'

'You said she wasn't the type,' Laura pointed out. 'Look here, I'll tell you what I'll do. I'll push over to Torbury myself after lunch and have a snoop round.'

'The police will have done that already, I expect.'

'Not until they've had a talk with you. You're the only direct source of information.'

'Oh, heck!' said Mark, dismayed. Like many boys of his age, he was afraid of policemen. He always imagined they might pounce on him for something done in school in which he had had no hand, and that the usual code would oblige him to take the rap and tell no tales. 'I can't tell them a single thing except what I've told you and my father and the manager, and none of it helps at all. I don't see,' he added, voicing his chief grievance, 'why it had to be *me* this happened to. We've *always* lost the teachers on school outings, and nothing has ever happened to any of them before, or to any of *us*, either!'

'I know,' said Laura sympathetically. 'But life's like that. You do a thing three hundred and ninety-nine times, and get away with it, and then, the four-hundredth time, you're in the mud up to the neck. It was always like that at school with me, and there never seemed any real reason. Come on. Let's get back. I want my elevenses. Besides, I can see a fair-weather crowd getting in, and I do hate sharing a raft with dozens of belly-flopping divers.'

The police interview, which was conducted by a quiet man in plain clothes, was not in the least distressing. Mark explained how he had been invited out by Miss Faintley and that he and his father had agreed (after some resistance on Mark's part) that the invitation must be accepted. Asked whether he had been surprised when he received the invitation, Mark replied that he *had*, and he had *not*, and clarified this by adding:

'I shouldn't have thought a lady teacher would want to take boys out in the hols., although some decent *masters* take you to France and Switzerland and Iceland and all that, but I wasn't much good at Miss Faintley's subject and fooled about a bit in form, so I should think she'd rather go out by herself when she had the chance. All the same, she was sort of educational – always improving our minds and being cultural and a lot of rot – so perhaps, as we were fairly near Torbury, and it's got a cathedral and some old city walls and a museum, she might have thought it a good thing to take me, although really I should have thought she'd rather have done some kind of a ramble and picked things for botany. That's supposed to be her subject.'

'In other words, you don't really know why you were invited out, and you didn't want to go.'

'Fair enough,' muttered Mark, shuffling a little and giving his father a half-glance.

'It's all right, son. I'm as sick as you are that I made you go,' said Mr Street. 'Will that be all, Inspector?'

'I'd just like a detailed description from Mark of how Miss Faintley was dressed, sir. He may have noticed some detail which I didn't get from the hotel porter who saw them go out.'

'Grey skirt, light-green blouse, dark-green cardigan, green-blue tweed jacket, no hat, dark-brown suede shoes, thick sort of stockings, gold wrist-watch on a thick gold bracelet thing . . . oh, and she'd put a ski-ing club badge in her lapel, two crossed skis and a circle of laurel leaves, but I don't think she was really entitled to wear it.'

'Why not?' asked the inspector. 'You've given me a first-rate description, and this bit about the badge and the wrist-watch may be extremely helpful. But why don't you think she was entitled to this ski-ing badge?'

'Well, Jenkins, who's rather gifted at getting the teachers to talk about their holidays when we're all getting browned-off in form, once asked Miss Faintley if she'd ever been in Switzerland, and Miss Faintley said she had never been nearer Switzerland than England.'

'She might have been in Norway,' the inspector pointed out. 'Now, one last question: has Miss Faintley any distinguishing mark? You see, she might lose her watch or this badge . . .'

'Or even her wig!' said Mark, by now at ease and beginning to giggle.

'. . . but a scar or a mole or a birthmark isn't so easy to lose,' the inspector gravely concluded. Mark sobered down.

'She hadn't got a scar, exactly,' he observed, 'but she had a little bald patch at the left side of her head about an inch and a half square. It was rather noticeable. She told us once that it was done in an air-raid when she was on an ack-ack site in the blitz. It got burnt, and the hair would never grow there again. So we didn't rot her about it, although Smalley told us afterwards that he betted Miss Faintley got it trying to rush into an air-raid shelter quicker than anyone else, and bumped her head.'

'What little toads boys are,' said the inspector, indulgently. 'Well, thank you, son. No doubt Miss Faintley will turn up like a shining penny before the morning. We're not really worried about her.' He winked at Mr Street. 'And if she had been a gentleman we shouldn't worry at all.'

Mark did not see why they should worry about ladies. There was to him, at his age, one definitely redundant sex.

'I'm sorry we lost each other,' he blurted out, 'but honestly, she wasn't in the bookshop where she'd *said* she'd be.'

'All right, sonny. We've got her home address. That's in the hotel register. So we can soon get to work on her relations to find out whether she went back home or not.'

'That is if anybody's there,' said Mark's father. 'So many of these single middle-aged women seem to live alone. But possibly she was in digs.'

'We'll soon know,' said the inspector. 'Meanwhile, don't you worry, sir. It wasn't the lad's fault, and I expect she'll turn up all right, although it was only correct of the manager here to let us know.'

CHAPTER THREE

LAURA

*

'Teach me to hear mermaids singing,
Or to keep off envy's stinging.
And find
What wind
Serves to advance an honest mind.'

JOHN DONNE – *Song*

BREAKFAST had been over for two hours and a half, and while the police officer had been questioning young Mark Street, Laura, and the sharp-eyed, yellow-skinned elderly lady with whom she had sat at table, had been for an exploratory walk along the cliffs and into the coves west of the bay where the two young people had bathed.

'Mrs Bradley, I could do with my elevenses,' observed Laura, when she and her employer came back to the eyrie of Cromlech village. 'What about coffee and buns?'

'Coffee for two, buns for one, and your valuable observations on the case of Street versus Faintley,' said Mrs Bradley with a grim cackle.

'That kid's worried,' said Laura. 'I told him I'd go to Torbury myself and have a look round, but it didn't really seem to ease his mind. I suppose that schoolmistress Faintley went off on a toot of some kind, but, if she did, it was hardly fair to take Mark along, do you think, to cover her questionable activities? Why *will* people try to remain respectable?'

'That question requires analysis, and, in any case, you mean respected, not respectable. Anyway, I have been talking to the boy's father. He declares that Miss Faintley was the last kind of person to do anything rash or to prove herself unreliable. He pictures her as an essentially serious-minded woman, not popular with the boys, but extremely anxious to do her best for them, and, of course, for the girls, too.'

'Parents often get weird ideas, though,' said Laura, unimpressed. 'I remember, when I was at school, we had a mistress whom everybody thought mousy and inoffensive in the extreme. There was an awful stink when it turned out that she had lifted all the school pots and shields and tried to pawn them. The pawnbroker brought them all back in a little handcart. She was found to be daffy, of course, but that only proves my point . . . that the parents and friends don't know everything. Shall you accompany me to Torbury?'

'No, child. The police will do everything in Torbury that is necessary. I shall take my knitting and sit on the cliff-top and enjoy the air.'

'*Not* your knitting,' said Laura. So Mrs Bradley went out for a walk, accompanied by a packet of chocolate, an ash-plant, and a Sealyham she did not know, but which elected to escort her on her way.

The determined Laura had an interview with Mark before she set out for Torbury. She wanted an exact description of Miss Faintley down to the smallest detail that Mark could remember. Mark repeated the description he had already given to the inspector and went off to play tennis with his father. Laura boarded a bus and nearly two hours later was in conversation with the assistant in the book-shop which Miss Faintley had stated she would visit whilst Mark was buying his film. She bought one of the new Penguins to add to her collection, but obtained no other satisfaction. The assistant had not noticed the lady Laura described, and had told the police so already.

'It's all right,' said Laura, with that air of frankness and innocent credulity which had got her out of many a tight place at school. 'It's really nothing on earth to do with me, but she was staying at my hotel, so naturally I'm rather interested. She seemed to be distinctly a bookworm, a quality to which I am partial. Are there any other book-shops in the town?'

She repeated her efforts at each of three more bookshops, received no help and went in search of some tea. Another thought struck her. Whatever else Miss Faintley had done she must have lunched somewhere. Laura wished she knew whether the woman was a restaurant, a good-pull-up or a pub-and-snack person. She might easily, of course, be a milk-bar devotee. In a city the size of Torbury it seemed hopeless to go to every place which offered rest and refresh-ment. There was one other possibility of tracing some of her movements, but, again, it offered only the remotest chance of success. If she were a smoker she might have gone into a tobacconist's shop. Unfortunately, not only was Tor-bury supplied all too liberally with tobacconists' shops but she had not thought of asking Mark whether Miss Faintley smoked. Possibly, however, he would not know.

It occurred to her that this could be remedied. She went into a public call-box and rang up the hotel. The call was answered from the office and she was told to hold on. The reply to her question came through quickly. The chamber-maid on Miss Faintley's floor had emptied an overflowing ashtray each time she tidied the room.

'Eureka!' said Laura, as she charged out of the telephone booth and returned to the bus station. From there she looked for the nearest tobacconist's, and discovered one next door but three to the chemist's at which Mark had purchased his film. The assistant recognized the description of Miss Faintley at once. She had bought a packet of twenty cigarettes, had paid with a pound note, and had asked the way to the railway station.

This was news indeed. Proud of her perspicacity, and the success which had at last attended it, Laura bought some cigarettes and went back to the bus stop. She boarded a bus which went to the station, and could not help wondering why Miss Faintley had not done the same thing. It seemed so very much more simple than asking the way in a shop. She knew, however, that she herself detested asking the way,

and only did so as a last resort or if she happened to be
badly pressed for time.

It took ten minutes for the bus to reach the station, and
during that ten minutes Laura thought hard. There seemed
no doubt that, if the tobacconist was right and it was Miss
Faintley who had asked the way to the station, then the
schoolmistress had abandoned Mark deliberately. The next
question was whether she had formed this intention before
or after leaving the boy at the chemist's. If she had already
decided to desert him when she issued the invitation at the
hotel, then Mark (for all that it had seemed to Laura a
highly unlikely theory at the time) might be right in supposing that he had been used as some kind of cover. Miss
Faintley must have been interested that some person or
persons should be misled into thinking that she intended
to spend the day out with the boy, when, in reality, she
proposed to travel by train to some destination at present
unknown.

On the other hand, if the invitation had been given in
good faith, then something must have happened in Torbury
to make Miss Faintley change her plans. She could not have
spoken to anybody on the bus; Mark would have mentioned
that. She must have met somebody immediately the boy left
her, and, in a very few minutes, rearranged her whole day
without attempting to contact him and let him know.

Of the two theories, Laura much preferred the first. It
was true that teachers, whichever their sex, were not apt to
take children out for the day and then abandon them, but
there was the practical question of time. Miss Faintley
would have had to meet this acquaintance, buy the cigarettes, inquire the way to the station and receive (judging
by the route Laura's bus was taking) a complicated answer,
if the second theory were to be tenable. Besides, Miss
Faintley had been out of sight by the time Mark came by
on that other bus on his way to the river, and all buses
travelled up that straight long street from the bus station,
past the chemist's, the bookshop and the tobacconist's,
because there was no other way for them to go, so if Miss

Faintley had been in the street Mark must have spotted her.

'Unless she was still in the tobacconist's when the kid came past on the bus . . . and, of course, most likely she was,' thought Laura at this point. 'And if she was, then the question of a time limit doesn't seem quite so important. Yet she'd know . . . or, at least, she'd *think* . . . that Mark would come looking for her, and might try the tobacconist's the moment he found she was not in the bookshop, so it wouldn't make a very good hidey-hole. Besides, Mark couldn't understand why Miss Faintley had offered to take him out. He was certain she couldn't have wanted to. I think that the boy (and that includes me and my first theory) guessed right the very first time!'

Still feeling the flush of detective fever, Laura got off the bus and went to inquire at the station. She did not obtain any information there. A main-line West Country station in August was too busy a place for much notice to have been taken of anybody unless he or she had provoked a breach of the peace.

There was one thing more that Laura could do. She took the return route to the bus station, walked back to the tobacconist and asked whether the woman she had described had been alone. The tobacconist had no idea, and looked at Laura rather oddly.

'I didn't know they came in plain clothes,' he said, not impudently but with a note of interrogation in his voice.

'Who?' Laura inquired.

'Policewomen.'

'Why shouldn't they? It's bound to be necessary sometimes.'

'I suppose so, when you come to think of it. What's she done, this woman?'

'Absconded. I can't tell you any more, you understand,' said Laura, picking up her cue, 'and she didn't speak to anybody in the shop except to you?'

'No. There wasn't any other person here.'

Satisfied that there was no useful purpose to be served

by remaining any longer in Torbury, and beginning to feel
the need of her dinner, Laura caught the next bus back to
Cromlech, and arrived at table to find Mrs Bradley just
finishing her soup. Mrs Bradley ordered wine, and asked
for an account of Laura's adventures.

'So I had better pass on to the police what I've found
out,' Laura concluded, 'but it's too late to bother about
that to-night, unless I tell them over the telephone, and
it doesn't really seem to amount to all that much, does
it?'

'You will probably find that they know it already,' said
Mrs Bradley, 'therefore I should not allow it to trouble you
until the morning. Enjoy your dinner, and afterwards we
will join the revellers in the hotel ballroom.'

By the time they rose from table the dining-room had
almost emptied. Laura was stopped on her way to the
lounge by Mark, who had been waiting for her to come out.

'Any luck?' he asked in the tone of one conspirator to
another.

'A bit. Miss Faintley did mean to leave you on your own
in Torbury. She went into a tobacconist's and asked the
way to the railway station.'

'Oh, that's *old* stuff! The police know that already. I
never thought of looking in the tobacco shop. I didn't know
she smoked. They can't find out where she went, though,
or even whether she took a ticket. If that's all you found
out I'm rather glad I didn't go with you. It was much better
fun staying here.'

Laura stared and then laughed.

'Well, I'm dashed!' she said. 'I wash my hands of the
business after that!'

But this she was not permitted to do. She woke at six
and raked Mark out for an early swim. He came willingly
enough, and on the way down to the sands he pointed out
to Laura the attractive path on the opposite side of the
bay.

'Bags we climb up there after bathing,' he said. 'The tide
was too high last time. I meant to do it then, but I couldn't

get round. It's nearly two hours later to-day. We might have done it yesterday morning, but there were too many people about. I've an idea it might be trespassing to go up there. I'm pretty certain there's a whacking big house just behind those trees.'

'If it's trespassing we must certainly have a stab at it,' said Laura warmly. 'I strongly object to this business of parts of the coast being cut off from public use and made into somebody's private property. Look here, I'll tell you what we'll do. We'll bathe from much farther along the beach so that the walk to the foot of those cliffs will be split in halves, so to speak. What do you say about that?'

They were fortunate enough to have the sea to themselves again, and when, invigorated and thoroughly lively, they were chasing one another along the firm sand at the edge of the sea, the landscape was still without figures, and they began the upward climb without meeting a soul. There was only one fly in the ointment. The path did not seem to be private, after all. A short sea-wall had been built to conserve the foot of the cliff, which was fairly soft and as rose-red as the legendary city, and there were steps in this wall to enable people to gain the zigzag path from the beach. It was obviously a public right of way.

Two turns of the path, and the sea was for a moment out of sight, for the path was between high bushes on which curled reddish stems of deep-scented, rich-toned honeysuckle. Here and there among the grass grew wild scabious, and, as the path mounted higher, came clumps of gorse and another glimpse of the sea.

'Well!' said Laura, taking out cigarettes and a piece of chocolate. 'I'm glad we came! Puff or suck?'

'Suck, please.' He accepted the chocolate gratefully and for a time they tramped silently upwards. Gulls in the huge cliffs perched on the dizzy ledges or plummeted through arcs of sky towards the sea. The bushes, except for the gorse, grew sparse and then ceased. Mark and Laura came out upon downland grasses where harebells grew and the birdsfoot trefoil was everywhere. There was spaciousness here. They were approaching the summit of the cliff, and the views to the east and west were again of horizon and coast.

'Grand!' said Mark. 'I wish we were trespassing, though.'

'We may be, in a minute or two,' said Laura. 'Unless my eyes deceive me, which, over this sort of thing, they seldom do, yonder looms a notice-board, and that of the baser sort, and I would risk a small and carefully-hoarded sum that on it appear the magic words we require.'

They strolled towards the board. It guarded a small stout gate which was strongly wired. In contrast to the bold and open headland, the owner of the gate had planted hawthorn hedges whose tops had weathered the gales but were now bent away from the sea. Any gaps in this formidable barrier . . . as Mark discovered by prowling . . . had also been fenced and wired.

'Blow!' said Mark, rejoining Laura, who was gazing speculatively at the enclosure. 'Without doing a frightful lot of damage (for which, I believe, you can be jugged), there doesn't seem a hope of getting in.'

'I've got an idea,' said Laura. 'Don't let's bother now, but we'll come out to-morrow morning and try from the other side. I've been thinking out the lie of the land, and I've some idea that you could work your way round to this point from that path which goes down by the side of the cliff-railway.'

'Shouldn't think so,' said Mark. 'I used that path yester-day while you were in Torbury, and all it does is to branch away under a tunnel. Then it comes out on the opposite side of the cliff-railway and beetles down to that road where cars can get down to the beach.'

'Eyes and no eyes,' said Laura severely. 'Your objective was simply the beach, therefore you did not see what *I* saw when I went along there after bathing on that first morning when you warned me about the tide. You wait, and after breakfast I'll show you. I'd thought of trying it by myself, but it's far more fun with the two of us.'

On the following morning they left the hotel again at six. Laura, accustomed to what she considered to be the dilatory opening of hotel front doors, had no scruples, at that hour of the morning, in breaking out of any place in which she happened to be staying. If the front door had a lock and the key was not there, she merely got out of a window in the lounge. Her argument was that at six in the morning all proper burglars were in bed and that therefore there was nothing anti-social in leaving a window open behind her.

At the *Whitesand*, however, the early-morning egress was simple. There were merely bolts top and bottom of the outer doors. The inner ones were swing doors and offered no obstacle. A short time later, Laura was wishing that it had not been easy, or, indeed, possible, to leave the hotel that morning.

She and Mark were again equipped for swimming, but this time they turned left instead of right along the front, and, coming to the cliff-railway, they crossed behind its upper platform and took a shaded ferny path of slopes and steps which ran alongside the railway track to about half-way down the cliff. Here the path proper, as Mark had pointed out, crossed the line by means of a tunnel, but there was also an ill-defined track which continued beside the line, and, instead of dipping, suddenly rose upwards to a shoulder of wooded hill.

It ended at a wall from which could be gained a view of the bathing beach below, but before the wall was reached there was a tremendously steep, bare scree which inclined at a desperate angle and offered a hare-brained chance of reaching a path below. Laura and Mark slipped, slithered and shot down this slope, and found themselves in a curiously shut-in little valley. On the farther side of it the entrancingly narrow path they had seen from above squeezed upwards between a wattle fence and some trees.

'Come on!' said Mark. 'This is good!'

The path climbed steeply but steadily until, at a sudden bend, it came out upon a wide, green space which reared at a stupefying gradient and showed a bent hedge at the top and a tiny gap in the hedge where the path went through.

Laura and Mark toiled onwards, their calf-muscles aching and their backs bent nearly double to assist them in clambering up. At the gap in the hedge the prospect of a further climb met them, but, in any case, there was a gate, and beyond the gate was a large bleak house, cut off from the open country by an iron railing of insurmountable aspect and most repellent mien which reinforced the bent hedge. There seemed no doubt that the owners of the house did not propose to have their privacy violated, for the gate, which was also of iron, showed the same unwelcoming face as the powerfully-constructed railings.

Laura and Mark stood at the gate and looked through. Mark gave the gate a slight shove, but it did not budge. Around the house were long-neglected flower-beds, weed-ridden and sprawling with nasturtium. The freely-flowering roses were small, and were choked by convolvulus and bindweed. Everywhere was the bright and deadly pink of the greater willow-herb.

In contrast to all this decay and obvious neglect, the path from the gate to the house had been carefully sanded. On its level greyish-brown surface there was never a footmark, although the surface here and there had been blown a little by the wind. Beyond that, the sand had not been disturbed, and it was obvious that it had not been laid down long.

'Queer sort of place,' said Mark. 'I shouldn't want to be about here much in the evening. Are we going to climb over the gate, or what?'

'We're in full view of some of the windows of that house,' Laura pointed out, 'and as there are curtains to one room it doesn't look as though the house can be empty. There is a caretaker living there, I should think. Still, having come so far, and the day being young, it seems a pity to go all that way back, so what I say is, let's take a pop and see what happens.'

They climbed over. The gate was not wired. They skirted the house, walking on the unkempt, weedy lawn. The garden on the other side was wild. The high bluff before them showed only the sky, with a gull turned to silver in the sun. When they got to the top the land dipped again, and they could see the wired hedge, and the post, and the back of that notice-board which they had resented two days earlier.

Mark went up to the board and gave the post a slight kick, but the post seemed firm in the earth and as he was wearing tennis shoes he merely hurt his toe. Laura was prowling along by the side of the hedge, looking for a thin place where possibly they might push their way through.

Suddenly she stopped. She had come to a dip in the ground and in the dip someone was lying. She could see that it was a woman, but her head was hidden in a gorse-bush, and there was something so odd in this as a choice of head-covering that Laura's heart thumped oddly and she felt sick. Regardless of the fact that she was on private property, she said urgently, 'Hi, you! Are you all right?'

There was no answer; neither (she knew) had she expected one. She looked back. Mark had swarmed up the post and was now clinging on to the notice-board and gazing out to sea. For the moment he seemed occupied, so Laura took out her towel, covered her hands with it to protect them as far as possible from the gorse prickles, and drew aside the bush.

The woman was dead. There was no doubt about that. The manner of her death was also apparent. A knife, of the type used by Commando troops during the war, had been thrust very neatly and cleanly into the side of her neck. Laura let the gorse fall back and was in time to intercept Mark, who had relinquished his impromptu crow's-nest and was so soft-footed in his tennis shoes that she had not heard him approach.

'Keep off,' said Laura. She held her towel, now full of gorse prickles, between Mark and the dead woman.

'Why, what's up?' asked Mark. He looked scared, and,

suddenly, very much younger than his age. 'It isn't Miss Faintley, is it?'

'Heavens, no!' said Laura, in a hearty, unnatural voice. 'Come on back, and make it slippy. No, look here, we can't spare all that time. We've got to break through this beastly hedge! Let's take up that post and use it as a ram! There's somebody ill in that dip. We must get some help. Look, Mark, do something for me. Get through this wretched hedge somehow, and go to our hotel for Mrs Bradley. She's a doctor. Ask her to come at once. Now, all hands to this beastly post!'

Her powerful muscles and Mark's co-operation soon had the post out of the ground. His swarming up it had loosened it. Mark at last charged his way through the hedge where the battering-ram of a post had aided exit, and, scratched, bleeding and breathless, ran down the zigzag path towards the sea. Laura waited until he was well down the slope, and then, with one last look at the body, which, from Mark's description, she felt certain was that of Miss Faintley, she walked slowly towards the house.

It was a fair-sized place, judging by the number of windows and the length of the side she went towards, but only the one window was curtained. She walked forward as quietly as she could, and peered in. There was nobody to be seen, so she knocked at the door, but, although she knocked again, and yet a third time, there was neither answer nor sound.

Laura tried the door, but it was either locked or bolted. Her excuse, if anybody came, was the body lying in the bushes, but she found that she needed no excuse. The house was most certainly empty. She peered in at other windows, went round to the kitchen entrance and knocked there, even shouted aloud in order to attract attention, but nothing came of any of this.

She returned to the body, but realized that by tramping about she might be destroying evidence, so, in the end, she returned to the notice-board which was now lying on the ground, a witness of her illegal behaviour. While she waited for Mrs Bradley she spent the time in widening the gap in the hedge. Then she crawled through it, sat on the cliff-top and stared thoughtfully out to sea. There was plenty to think about. Miss Faintley inquiring for Torbury railway station, and Miss Faintley dead on top of the Cromlech cliffs did not seem to make sense until it occurred to Laura that Miss Faintley had not intended to travel by train, but had had an appointment to meet someone at the station.

'And he brought her up here and did for her,' Laura concluded. 'Must be one of those insane sex crimes. How deadly dull, and how horrible!'

Mrs Bradley arrived with Mark as guide, crawled through the gap which Laura had considerably enlarged, and sent Mark back to breakfast.

'And now, child,' she said briskly, 'what have we here?'

Laura took her to the spot.

'Hm!' said Mrs Bradley, rising after she had examined the wound. 'A very pretty piece of work, neat, skilful and clean. She was killed somewhere else ... on that newly-sanded path, we may conclude, unless other evidence is forthcoming. You had better go at once for the police. I'll stay here until they come. I presume, from the clothing, that this is Miss Faintley. I take it that Mark has not seen the body?'

'No, I took care of that, of course,' said Laura. She nodded, and bounded away.

Mrs Bradley knelt down again as soon as Laura had disappeared. There was something more interesting than at first she had thought about the weapon. She took out the small magnifying glass which she invariably carried, and examined all that she could see of the knife. Almost the full length of the blade had been driven home, but she was able to examine the way in which the top of it met the hilt. The knife was not of the Service type, after all. It was, although a neat and powerful job, home-made. Well-forged and even handsome though it was, there was still no doubt that the work had never been done by Wilkinson's.

She doubted whether this fact would help the police very

much. Private manufacturers of lethal weapons do not usually advertise their wares, and it was unlikely, she thought, that the murderer's fingerprints would be on record.

CHAPTER FOUR

DETECTIVE-INSPECTOR VARDON

*

'O they have hunted in good green-wood
The back* but and the rae,*
And they've drawn near Brown Robin's bow'r
About the close of day.'
                    Border Ballad – *Rose the Red and White Lily*

'AND you never saw her before, Miss Menzies?' inquired Detective-Inspector Vardon (Dolly to his intimates).

'Never before.'

'Yet you were staying at the same hotel here in Cromlech?'

'Yes, of course. But the only time I could have seen her was at breakfast on the first morning of my stay, and, as it happens, I went out for an early swim and by the time I had got back to the hotel, and made myself presentable for breakfast, Miss Faintley had left the dining-room.'

'How do you know that?'

'Mark Street pointed out her table later on. I suppose, that first morning, Miss Faintley had gone up to get ready for their outing.'

'Yes?'

'Miss Faintley was not in to lunch that day, of course. She had gone with Mark to Torbury. She did not come back to the hotel.'

'Thank you, Miss Menzies. Now, if you had never seen Miss Faintley, what made you come to the conclusion that the dead body you found was hers?'

'Be yourself, Inspector,' urged Laura reproachfully. 'I

* Buck, roe.

guessed it was Miss Faintley because of the way she . . . it
. . . was dressed – Mark had described her to me before I
went into Torbury – and partly because I knew Miss
Faintley was missing and that you had been inquiring
about her from the Street family.'

'How was it that you came upon the body?'

'I was trespassing.'

'Oh, you do realize that you had no business to be up
there?'

'I don't agree at all about that,' replied Laura with spirit.
'I contend that if selfish people mark off part of the coast
as their private property they deserve to have trespassers
and worse. Not litter-fiends, though,' she added hastily. 'I
do bar those at all times.'

'I understand that you had climbed over into a garden.
That, surely, was a different kind of trespass. You will be
required to give evidence at the inquest, of course. You'll
be prepared for that, won't you? Finding the body, you
know.'

He left her and tackled Mark again. Mark, although
slightly uneasy, was feeling that he had a place in the sun.
For once he would be the chief *raconteur* at school. He
almost longed for the holidays to be over so that he could
be there to tell the tale. 'I realized at once it must be old
Semi-Conscious.' (No, better say Miss Faintley now.) 'The
clues led unerringly to the canyon. I had trailed her for
miles up hills where only the toughest and most determined
would have ventured, and my keen eye discerned her at
once where she lay in the shadow of an enormous bluff. . . '
(No, somehow, the style, although satisfying, was not quite
his. Some fool was sure to butt in with some silly question
before he got half as far as that.) He was recasting his
account of the affair when the Inspector sent for him.

'Hullo, Mark. Sit down. Now, listen. Whose idea was it
that you and Miss Menzies took that early walk and found
Miss Faintley dead?'

'Sorry, not a clue,' said Mark. 'I don't think it was
anyone's idea. We just simply went, that's all.'

'Miss Menzies' idea,' wrote the Inspector in his shiny little notebook. 'Right, Mark. Where were you when Miss Menzies found the body?'

'I was . . . ' (Fingerprints? Better tell the truth! They're sure to know!) 'I was, well, actually, I was climbing a post.'

'A post?'

'Yes, well, the post with the notice-board on it. You know . . . "Trespassers will be Dealt With".'

'Dealt with?'

'That's what it said. We had read it from the other side the day before. It got us sort of mad, so we thought we'd try to get in the other way round.'

'How did you discover that there *was* another way round? You've never stayed here before. Your father said so.'

Mark looked scared. He was determined neither to flatter nor to let down Laura by declaring that hers had been the moving spirit in the adventure, and the Inspector's question flustered him. Into his desperation an idea came hurtling like a life-line.

'Well, you see,' he said, 'I felt sure there was a house up there somewhere, and they'd have to have grub, and perhaps they kept a car, and all that. There'd have to be some other way in, so we thought we'd look for it.'

'I see. You thought you'd look for it. Very reasonable, especially as you'd never been there before.'

This put Mark on his guard. When parents and teachers agreed with you, that was the time to keep your eye skinned. It stood to reason that they did not agree with you really. They always had something up their sleeve. He hedged.

'It just seemed like that,' he said. 'Miss Menzies wouldn't see it that way, I don't suppose. She just wanted to get down to the beach. There's the cliff railway, of course, but it wasn't running so early, and we wanted our bathe, and it seemed such a sweat, going back all that way, or so we thought.'

'I see. Thank you, Mark. Going in for the law, by any chance?'

He departed, grinning. He left Mark feeling uneasy. To

add to this uneasiness, on his way upstairs Mark encountered the yellow-skinned Mrs Bradley. He stood aside
politely at the turn of the flight to let her pass, and trusted
that he would escape notice, but, instead of passing him,
she stood still and they met face to face.

'Well, Sir Gareth!' she said cheerfully. 'How does the
Lady Lyonours to-day?' Mark looked and felt embarrassed
and would have tried to slip past had he been even one year
younger. As it was, he stood his ground like a man. He
blushed and said:

'All right, I expect. After you. It's unlucky to pass on the
stairs.'

'I think that our paths *should* cross,' said the ancient
lady. 'What is this trouble in which you have involved my
secretary, amanuensis, and friend, Miss Laura Menzies?
Account to me for the fact that you have set the blood-
hounds on her trail.'

'But I didn't!' said Mark indignantly, his voice shrill
with fright. 'In fact ... as a matter of fact ... well, that
policeman jolly well third-degreed me, but I wasn't going
to give Laura away!'

'Come with me.' She led the way upstairs to her lair.
'In here. Sit down. Comfort you with apples' – she produced
sweets and a bottle of orange juice – 'stay you with flagons,
although neither of us, thank goodness, is sick of love.'

Mark nervously took a sweet and accepted the drink she
poured out.

'I don't know anything about Miss Faintley, I swear I
don't,' he said. Mrs Bradley clicked her tongue.

'Who mentioned Miss Faintley?' she demanded. 'No, my
dear Solomon, Miss Faintley is beside the point at the
moment. Tell me about your school.'

'School? But I thought Miss Faintley – '

'Quite so. Whose form are you in?'

'Mr Bannister's.'

'What manner of man may he be?'

'He's all right,' said Mark, keeping his guard up.

'What is his standing in the school?'

'He doesn't stand much. He sits, and fetches you out in the front.'

'With what in mind? Are his intentions honourable?'

'Oh, he's all right,' repeated Mark. 'Sometimes it's your work, and he marks it and perhaps he keeps you in, and sometimes it's the cane, and then you don't get kept in, but nobody really grouses. He takes us for football sometimes.'

'Ah! Nobody really grouses. A school of philosophers, I find. Now, what subject . . . no, never mind that at the moment, although I confess that I do not at present perceive the answer to what I was about to ask you. Now, Mr Plato, how many women teachers are there in the school?'

'Well, there's Mrs Rolls, Miss Ellersby, Miss Franks, Miss Batt, Miss Welling and Miss Cardillon. That's all, except . . . well, Miss Faintley, of course. And, if you want to know, she takes us for Nature – it's a sort of botany really.'

'And the head-teacher's name?'

'Miss Golightly.'

'A woman, eh?'

'Worse luck!' said Mark. He scowled. 'She favours the girls.'

'A woman of character, I feel. Another bite of the serpent's tooth, dear Daniel?' She handed over a dish and Mark accepted some chocolate.

'I thought it was *lions* with Daniel,' he observed, 'not serpents. We had a poem . . . "*Bite* Daniel!" Rather good.'

'Not only serpents, but every creeping thing,' his terrifying hostess observed. 'Did Miss Faintley teach zoology?'

'No, botany and nature study. Tadpoles, and twigs and things, and bees and pollen, and that rot. I shall be jolly glad when I go up into the next form. Then we have Mr Roberts for science and do decent experiments and visit the gas-works and all that. He made the school a television set last term.'

'What does Mr Bannister teach?'

'Maths.'

'And is it a favourite subject with you? I feel that as Mr Bannister is your form-master – '

'It's all right. I like geometry better than algebra. You can fool about with protractors and set-squares and things, and – '

'No doubt with compasses, too?'

Mark wriggled, as one who not only suspected irony but had recollected the stab of an ancient wound.

'You can't do much with Mr Bannister in that way,' he replied. 'Not if he's in the room. It all goes on when he goes out.'

'And his outings, I swear, are not frequent. But he takes the boys for football, therefore much is forgiven him.'

'Yes, on Saturday mornings. I don't think he's got much to do with his time. I meet him sometimes, mooching about, but he has jolly decent holidays, I believe. Not like' – he scowled at the recollection of Ellison and the fun they had planned to have in France – 'not like at Cromlech, where there's nothing to do except bathe.'

'What sort of holidays would *you* call good ones?'

'Well, I'd planned to go to France, these hols., with a friend of mine.'

'Boy or girl?'

'*Girls* are no good. I don't mean Laura, but, then, she's not a girl. She's pretty old, I should think.'

Mrs Bradley, who looked upon her secretary as a child, gravely conceded that Laura was in the sere and yellow leaf, and added:

'France is a beautiful country, and I am not surprised that your plans included a visit there. Does Mr Bannister like France?'

'I expect so. He's been into those prehistoric caves. Lascaux, they're called, I think. They're in the south-west somewhere.'

'Lascaux, yes. So have I. *The Jumping Cow* and so forth.'

'Mr Bannister says it isn't. It wouldn't be jumping at all, except that the artist didn't want to cover up the ponies that some earlier bloke had drawn, so he put its legs up.'

'The cow jumped over the moon, according to popular legend. What thought he of the Apocalyptic Beast, on the main hall vaulting?'

'I don't know. He didn't mention that one. It comes in *Revelations*, doesn't it?'

'And the beast which I saw was like unto a leopard, and his feet were as the feet of a bear, and his mouth as the mouth of a lion,' quoted Mrs Bradley.

'Yes, I expect that's the bit. He showed us pictures in a book he'd bought.* There's an awfully good one of a horse slipping over a precipice and another of some deer crossing a stream. He doesn't often tell us things about his holidays, like some of the masters do, but he did tell us about how five French chaps lost their dog and found the caves. There was a hole where a tree had blown down, and I suppose the dog fell in the hole and the chaps went after it. I bet they were jolly surprised when they found themselves in that whacking big place with all those paintings on the walls! I bet it's weird in there, isn't it?'

'Extremely weird.'

'If my people hadn't turned sticky about France, Ellison – he's my friend – and I were going to cycle to Lascaux and have a look for ourselves.'

'A worthy object of pilgrimage. I wonder whether Miss Faintley ever told you how she spent *her* holidays?'

'We wouldn't have been very interested in *ladies'* holidays. They don't often do much that you'd want to hear about, do they?'

'Alas, no. Mine is a dull and deficient sex, I fear.'

Mark looked alarmed, and began to sidle towards the door. Mrs Bradley smiled like a well-intentioned serpent and let him go. Mark walked straight into the Inspector.

'Ah, Mark! The very man!' said Vardon, with what, to Mark, sounded like satisfaction of a ghoulish and frightening kind. 'Come into the little writing-room – there's nobody there – and tell me all about your school.'

Except for the bit concerning Mr Bannister and the

Lascaux: A Commentary – Alan Houghton Brodrick.

Aurignacian wall-paintings (which he did not think Vardon would find interesting, even supposing that he had ever heard of them), Mark stolidly repeated the information he had given to Mrs Bradley.

'So Miss Faintley taught nature study, did she? What was she down this way for? – to collect specimens for next term's work?'

'I haven't a clue,' said Mark doggedly. 'Why don't you look at her luggage and see if she'd brought her botanical cases with her? They're kind of tin things. Airtight, I think, when they're fastened. They're jolly expensive, I believe, because Jones fell off his bike once when she'd lent him one to take home some specimens after a nature ramble . . . it wasn't bad: old Skipton got chased by a bull . . . and when Jones fell off his bike this botany case got itself dented and Miss Faintley moaned like billy-o when he took it back to her on Monday morning. He apologized, too, and, after all, he *had* done his knee in for games.'

'And what were these rambles? What was their object? . . . just anything you kids picked up, or for anything special?'

Mark looked round as Mrs Bradley came into the small room.

'Well, she'd let us take anything we liked, I suppose, but ferns and things were her favourites. Old Bewston nearly broke his neck climbing down an old quarry one Saturday. It wasn't bad fun when that sort of thing happened, of course, but mostly it was just punk, and we used to chase the girls with toads to get a bit of life into things.'

'What's the name of the headmaster, Mark?'

'It isn't. It's a her.'

'Woman head of a mixed school, eh?' said the Inspector. He wrote it down. 'What's she like? A man-eater?'

'She's all right,' muttered Mark.

'What's her name?'

'Miss Golightly.'

'And does she?'

Mark, who related flippancy with sarcasm and therefore

distrusted it, made no reply. He stared at the pattern on the rug, then raised his eyes and asked abruptly:

'Do you *know* yet who murdered Miss Faintley?'

'Not yet,' the Inspector replied, 'but it's only a question of time, laddie. You didn't, I suppose, see anybody up at that house?'

'I didn't go to the house,' said Mark regretfully. 'And your police won't have me up there, because I've tried.'

The house, it seemed, was an enigma. Inquiry showed that it had been built by a certain Colonel Arden who, at one time – about 1901 the *savants* thought – had occupied it in company with his wife and two daughters. After his death it had remained empty for several years and had been up for sale. Then, in 1914, the Army had had it, and when that war was over it had been bought by a private school but was found unsuitably dangerous for small boys because of its position on the top of the cliff. It had been put up for sale again without success. The police interviewed the owner and his agents, but could gain no further information.

'And that's as far as we can get,' said Inspector Vardon when he had journeyed to the town of Kindleford, where Miss Faintley had lived. He was speaking to his opposite number at the Kindleford police station. 'What can you tell us about this woman Faintley?'

'Nothing much,' replied Inspector Darling. 'I've recently heard that she had some connexion with a small tradesman in one of the back streets here, a fellow we've never caught out, but have had our eye on for some time. We've an idea he's a fence, but we've never been able to prove anything. Of course, she may have been coshed and robbed. You can't rule that out in these days.'

'It wasn't robbery,' said Vardon. 'Her handbag was near the body and contained three pounds and some silver and coppers. The rest of her money she had given in at the hotel office for safe keeping.'

'The murderer may have been disappointed with his haul and clocked her in a fit of temper.'

'Could be, but she was wearing a pretty good wrist-watch on a wide gold bracelet. Must be worth every bit of thirty or forty pounds.'

'Um, yes. You'd think he'd take that. Well, what about going along to her home? I don't think it will help much, though. She lived with an aunt, whom I've already interviewed, but I expect you'd like to talk to her for yourself.'

The aunt was a gaunt, sallow woman in her sixties. She seemed less grieved than annoyed by her bereavement, Vardon thought.

'And who's to pay the rent, or where I'm to go, is more than I can fathom,' she said at the end of half an hour's conversation during which she had told them nothing of any value. 'When I came here to be a companion to Lily I never thought of being left with the place on my hands like this. Naturally I expected to go first.'

'How long have you lived here, Miss Faintley?'

'Only since Lily joined the school. We couldn't get anything cheaper, and she never much liked the idea of lodgings. Always used to her own home until it was blitzed and her mother died, my brother having died several years before, of course, and Lily her mother's sole support except for the pension.'

'Did they live in London, then?'

'Yes. After the house was blitzed they were given a requisitioned one, but my sister-in-law was very hard to please and never liked it.'

'Oh, she wasn't killed when their home was destroyed?'

'No, neither of them was hurt, except the shock. But Mattie never got over the loss of her furniture and that. She brooded. I used to get cross with her and tell her she owed it to Lily to brace herself up, but it seemed she couldn't bring herself. She died the year before last, and Lily tried lodgings and didn't like them, so she persuaded me to bring my bits of things and we set up here. She'd nothing of her own except a bookcase and her writing-desk and chair, and those *precious* botanical cases which I believe have been more than half the trouble. I gave up my little house to do her a favour, and I shall never be able to get it back with the shortage like it is. I don't know *what* I shall do!'

'How long did your niece expect to stay at Cromlech for her holiday this year?'

'That's what's so strange. I don't know what she was doing in Cromlech at all! I mean, what *is* there in a place like that? We had a very nice private hotel booked in Torbury, where there would at least have been a picture palace if it turned wet, and a theatre if you wanted to fill up your evenings! But Cromlech hasn't even a pier . . . just the beach huts and the cliff-railway. I was to have joined her in Torbury next week, and I was looking forward to it very much, my life being what you see . . . this flat, and the shopping, and Lily's meals, and the washing. So why she was staying at a hotel in Cromlech is more than I can fathom. If she'd been younger, or the flighty kind, I would have thought the worst, for she's never been as open with me as you would have thought, living together as we did and me having nobody to talk to for hours on end, but one thing I did know about her, she had no use for men of any sort and at any time. She thought herself a cut above them . . . most of them, anyway.'

Darling was tempted to refer to the cases of Miss Camille Clifford and other ladies whom their friends would not have supposed capable of some of the erratic and inexplicable emotions which had led to their being murdered, but he held his peace, hoping that something would pop up in the aunt's whining, complaining monologue which would give a clue to Miss Faintley's murderer.

He was not nearly as certain as the aunt professed to be that there was not a love-affair at the bottom of the mystery. The fact, that, unknown to her aunt, Miss Faintley had purposed to stay in Cromlech when she was supposed to be staying in Torbury, was very significant, he thought. He glanced at Vardon. Vardon drummed on the table for a moment, and then asked:

'Did you receive a letter from your niece after she left here?'

'A postcard, not a letter. I would always like to know she'd arrived safely. Trains are such funny things nowadays, what with accidents and assaults and the drivers not stopping at the right stations and not troubling to look at the signal-boxes and always grumbling when they have to spend a night away from their wives. I never *did* think British Railways would work, and, of course, they don't. I always used to like the old G.W.R. You could trust the G.W.R. as I always said.'

'And have you kept the postcard?' asked Vardon, damming the stream, or, possibly, blocking the track.

'Oh, yes, I've got it. I shall always keep it now, of course, it being Lily's last words. You won't want to take it away with you, will you?'

'I should just like to see it.'

'It's postmarked Torbury all right, if that's what you mean. Think of the deceitfulness, if she was really at Cromlech!'

She brought the card. The postmark was indeed Torbury, so there was not much doubt but that Miss Faintley had not intended to allow her aunt to know that she had spent any nights in Cromlech. Still, that was not evidence of any criminal intention.

'It wouldn't do if our relatives had to know everything we got up to,' said Vardon soothingly. 'We're all entitled to a bit of private life sometimes. Don't mean there's any harm in it, although, in this case, it's turned out very distressing indeed. You said your niece was living somewhere else in Kindleford before you took over her housekeeping, didn't you? I'd better have the address of those lodgings.' He took it down. 'How long was your niece there?'

'A matter of three weeks. She didn't like it there at all. No home comforts, and she had to eat with the family, which didn't suit her ladyship at all.'

'Looks like a job for the Yard if the young woman had London connexions,' said Vardon when the two officers had returned to Kindleford police station. 'I don't suppose they'll be able to tell us anything helpful at the school here.'

'Trouble is that the schools are all on holiday. It's hard to get hold of anybody, even if they *could* be of use. What about trying the Education Office?'

'Better than nothing, but, all the same, a dead end, I expect.'

The Education Office proved to be an annexe to the Town Hall. The Education Officer was on holiday, but his deputy, an alert woman of about thirty, was able to assure the police that, so far as the Education Office was concerned, they knew nothing about Miss Faintley except the formal matters relating to her employment and could suggest nothing which would help an investigation into the circumstances of her sudden death.

Vardon went next to the lodgings which Miss Faintley had occupied. They were at a terrace house in one of the better streets of Kindleford, but were drab and depressing. The landlady, a tall female whose appearance was not improved by her dust-cap and overall, was prepared with two observations. She had never liked Miss Faintley from the first, and she had always said that those stuck-up ones came off the worst in the end.

Vardon, disregarding these remarks, which were prejudiced, he felt, by the fact that Miss Faintley had not remained longer in the lodgings, inquired concerning Miss Faintley's friends and acquaintances.

'Oh, she'd have one and another in to tea, and sometimes she went on a hike or to the pictures.'

'Were the "one-and-another" men or women friends?'

'Well, come to think of it, there has only ever been the one – a Miss Franks from the school. They seemed to be very thick, her and Miss Faintley did, though what they saw in each other – '

'No men friends, so far as you know, then?'

'There's them that can get men friends of the right sort, which is the marrying kind, and them that can get 'em of the wrong sort, which is what I prefer not to name, and

there's some can't get 'em of any sort, and that was Miss
Faintley.'

The landlady's contempt was obvious. Vardon thanked
her for her information, and returned to the aunt to put the
same questions.

There *was* a Miss Franks, the aunt agreed. She had
been once or twice to visit them, but had seemed rather
Red in her ideas, her being the art teacher, so the older
Miss Faintley had warned the younger Miss Faintley that
(whether they had the moral right to do so or not) Education Committees were conditioned to take a poor view of
such people. The younger Miss Faintley had taken the hint,
her aunt thought, and nothing more had been seen of Miss
Franks at the flat.

Consumed by impatience, Vardon longed for the end of
the school's summer vacation. He decided that if Miss
Franks could not help him, probably nobody could. There
remained the headmistress. Vardon wondered whether it
might be possible to find her at the school engaged in the
composition of time-tables for the coming term. He was
unlucky. The only people he encountered were the caretaker and a couple of cleaners.

'Miss Faintley?' said the caretaker, a lean, sardonic man
of forty-five. 'Yes, I saw the notice in the papers. Ever
served in a mixed battery, Inspector? Always the ones
nobody ever thought of who pick up all the trouble. The
real floozies never cop out. It's the amateurs buy it, sir . . .
always.'

'So Miss Faintley was what one might call the typical
schoolmistress, eh?'

'There's no such thing as a typical schoolmistress.
Colonel's lady and Judy O'Grady . . . that's what they are.
And what they are under their skins only the kids know . . .
and, like God, *they* won't let on, not to *you* they won't.'

'You don't know, of course, where I could get in touch
with the headmistress?'

'I do not, sir. Caravannin' on the Continent is Miss
Golightly, with a couple of lady friends. They're on the

move every day. She'll be in school a couple of days before the openin' day of term, according to her usual custom, but apart from that, she can't be got at nohow.'

He sounded extremely well satisfied with this fact and repeated it, adding that if Vardon knew the Education Office as Butters knew it, he would not be surprised at nothing, and Miss Golightly, she was one with her head screwed on, was Miss Golightly.

Vardon, disgruntled, returned to the police station. Suddenly he said to Darling:

'You mentioned a young chap told you that Miss Faintley had had some dealings with a fellow you think may be a fence. That sounds an unlikely sort of game for a schoolmistress. Was the chap sure?'

'Quite sure. Tell you what; I'll send for him and you can talk to him for yourself. I think he'll convince you. I'll stake my reputation he's telling the truth.'

Mandsell, brought to the police station in a car which had a plain-clothes driver, was briefly introduced by Darling. He saw a big man with a genial appearance and lips which indicated a sense of humour. Vardon saw a medium-sized, rather shabby, likeable young man whose accent betrayed his place of learning.

'What can I do for you, Inspector? I've already told all I know to Mr Darling.'

'Quite so, sir.' The West Country voice was soothing. 'It's just that I'd like your story at first-hand. Can I have your full name and address for my records?'

'George Geoffrey Madeston Mandsell. I lodge with a Mr and Mrs Deaks at 31 Upper Bridge Street. I'm a writer.'

'Very good, sir. And now . . .'

'I decided to go out for a walk at about half-past eight on the evening of July 25th. I was going to the library. I'd forgotten it was closed on Thursdays. On my way home I went into the telephone-box half-way along Park Road. I only went in to look up a number, but the telephone buzzed and I picked up the receiver.'

'Why did you do that, sir?'

'I don't know. It was subconscious, just a natural reaction. The voice at the other end was Miss Faintley's, or so it said. It seems as if somebody had made an arrangement that she was to ring up that box at that particular time. People do that sometimes, I believe, if they don't want to be overheard or if one of them isn't on the phone. I tried to explain who I was, and that I'd seen a man leave the box a minute before I got there, but she wouldn't listen.'

'Oh? You think you saw the man who was to have been her correspondent?'

'Well, I can't be sure of that, of course, but it seemed rather likely.'

'Can you describe him?'

'No, I'm afraid I can't. He was about my height, I should say, and youngish . . . that is to say, probably in his thirties. He had his back to me as he left the box. His hat was pulled down and his coat-collar was right up. I guessed he was youngish because of the rate at which he walked.'

'What did Miss Faintley have to say? It must have seemed to her very important if she would not let you explain who you were.'

'I don't know how important it was, really. The only thing I do know is that she seemed in the deuce of a hurry to get the conversation over because there were people about who might come in and overhear her end of it.'

'And what was her end of it?'

'She wanted this man, whoever he was, to get a parcel from Hagford railway station and take it to a man called Tomson.'

'Yes, sir?'

'Well, the next bit may sound rather silly, but, not having much to do next day, I walked over to Hagford, picked up the parcel and bunged it in.'

'Why?'

'Same reason as that for which I took the telephone call, I suppose. I can't really explain it. It just seemed fun at the time and something to do.'

'Very well, sir. Thank you for your information. You

won't be changing your lodgings at present, sir, I take it?'

'No, I don't think so. Why?'

'Just that we should like to have you around, sir. Your evidence may be very important indeed. Which way was the man going?'

'Oh, away from the direction of the High Street, but, of course, he'd disappeared by the time I came out of the box.'

'What do *you* make of him?' asked Vardon, when Mandsell had gone.

'Quite as innocent as he sounds. I wonder what made him go and fetch that parcel, though? It's a ten-mile tramp there and back.'

'Curiosity, I expect. He's a writer. They're usually a bit romantic in their outlook and do things other people wouldn't think of doing.'

'Maybe that's it. What interests me most is that the parcel had to be delivered to old man Tomson. I told you we'd had our eye on him for receiving. I've already looked him up, of course, but come along and see what you make of him. First-hand impressions are always best.'

The shop was not very clean. That was the first thing which struck Vardon when the two inspectors walked in. The proprietor was alternately obsequious and insolent, but Darling had been prepared for that. He had met Tomson before.

'Take in parcels? Why, no, sir, not with the post office so close. The only thing I do in that line is Small Ads.'

'Quite so,' said Vardon. 'What about a Small Ad. from a lady named Faintley?'

The proprietor appeared to reflect. Then his face brightened.

'Miss Faintley? Well, yes, but that was not a Small Ad. That was a cry from the heart.'

'Love letters?'

'I couldn't say, but I took in a matter of a dozen letters or more in the past three months, all addressed in the same writing.'

'When did the last of them come?'

'Let me see, now. Yes, the last of them came on 23rd July. But that's easy understandable. She went on holiday after that.'

'I see. And no doubt presents were delivered as well as letters?'

'Not so far as I know. I've told you I don't take parcels.'

'I think there were parcels, Tomson. And one of them came to Hagford just before Miss Faintley went on holiday. A young fellow delivered it to you under Miss Faintley's instructions and you refused to give him a receipt.'

'All right! Have it your own way! There *was* a parcel, then! But he didn't ask for a receipt. He asked for five pounds.'

'And you gave it him?'

'At the point of a gun, what would *you* do?'

'So he had a gun?'

'He put his hand in his jacket pocket and threatened me. That's all I know. I didn't resist. I don't pretend to be a blinking hero.'

'You'd probably pretend very badly,' put in Darling, excusably. 'All right, Tomson. Watch your step, that's all. Not that you need the advice. I've had *two* independent bits of information about you and the things you get up to.'

'You'll be a long time putting salt on *that* bird's tail,' said Vardon, grinning, when they left.

'You wait and see,' retorted Darling. 'Now I *know* he's up to something fishy I'll soon be able to pull him in, and when I do he'd better come clean. I'll bet he's got no alibi for Miss Faintley's murder.'

'What was the other information you told him you had?'

'Oh, merely corroborative evidence that Miss Faintley did have some connexion with him. Came from a chap I know pretty well – one of the masters at the school. Doesn't give any clue to the murder, worse luck, but it makes Mandsell's story quite credible. She *did* have some connexion with Tomson, and a fishy connexion, too. She'd taken parcels to him from Hagford before, *and* got a smack across the chops for her pains!'

'Sounds as if she was married to him!'

'The aunt would have known that, I should think! But it argues a queer situation between shopkeeper and customer, all the same!'

CHAPTER FIVE

DETECTIVE-INSPECTOR DARLING

*

'. . . and now let us take a walk a little way out of the town.'

THE BROTHERS GRIMM – *The Dog and the Sparrow*

BUT, in spite of these words, Detective-Inspector Darling was dissatisfied. Crime, in Kindleford, was of the dull, unrewarding kind. Offensive parking of cars on the wrong side of the High Street on Wednesdays and Fridays – Friday was market day in Kindleford – petty larceny in which the culprit (bone-headed, in the detective-inspector's opinion) was only too easily distinguishable; an occasional misinterpretation of the licensing laws, were all the grist which had ever come to his mill until the extraordinary death, on holiday, of this obscure, inoffensive (so far as he knew or was concerned), little-known, unattractive school-marm.

He was not an unduly ambitious officer, but he had often longed for a case which would make headlines in the big newspapers. He had often longed for a case of murder. It had come his way, but for all the good it did him it might as well never have happened, he considered. The murder, although it was the murder of one of Kindleford's residents, had had the tactlessness to take place in another county. His co-operation was vital to the police of that county, but instead of being in a position to take fingerprints, photograph the body, make brilliant deductions from the medical evidence and arrest the wrongdoer in a flood of limelight, the only thing he could do was to badger, respectively, a rather elderly lady, aunt to the deceased Miss Faintley, a young, impecunious, obviously innocent author and a miserable little rat of a shopkeeper, who had probably told him already everything he knew. He decided to leave the aunt alone and to concentrate first on Mandsell.

The author seemed pleased with life and welcomed him cordially, although a fountain-pen in his hand and an ink-smudge on his nose indicated that he was busy with composition.

'I've sold a short story,' he said, 'and do you know what I've based it on?'

'I couldn't begin to guess, sir, unless on the tale of Miss Faintley's mysterious parcel. And that being so – '

'I've told you all I know,' said Mandsell hastily, 'so I didn't see why I shouldn't make use of the idea. It couldn't possibly matter to anyone else.'

'I'm not so sure of that, sir. After all, the fact remains that you accepted this parcel from Hagford, delivered it to Tomson in Miss Faintley's name, did not get a receipt, and then we learn of the death of Miss Faintley, to whom the parcel was addressed.'

'You can't say it was the result of what I did ... her death, you know. She was killed on holiday. There's nothing on earth to connect her death with the parcel.'

'Not necessarily, sir, I agree, but, so far as we can see, these parcels were a bit of a mystery. You wouldn't care to hazard a guess what was in the one you carried?'

'I haven't a clue. I wish I had. I'm pretty sure it was wooden – it was very firm, you know, not just brown paper and string – and I know it was rather like a photograph, but that's as much as I can tell you.'

'You acted very rashly, sir, in deciding to undertake this little commission. Tomson is by way of being a marked man.'

'Yes, but I couldn't know that. What I did was more or less as a joke.'

'Very likely, sir. We are quite prepared to accept that explanation. But now, sir, this walk you took on a very wet, unpleasant evening.'

'Yes, I was worried. I was rather exercised in my mind about my royalties.'

'In other words, you were on the rocks, sir. That's what we understand from your landlady. Then, suddenly, on the following day, you found yourself in a position to pay her four pounds.'

Mandsell, who had not thought fit to disclose this fact, looked apprehensive.

'Well, that wasn't very much, was it?' he said belligerently.

'You wouldn't care to tell me how you came into the possession of the four pounds, sir?' The Inspector's voice was persuasive but his eye was keen.

'I didn't steal it, if that's what you mean!'

'Of course I don't mean that, sir. We know where it came from, and you would do better to trust us. Now, about you and Miss Faintley and the telephone conversation. Haven't you any idea *at all* as to the identity of the gentleman that walked away down Park Road just before you arrived at the telephone-box?'

'Not a clue. It was raining hard, you know, and, as I think I told you, his coat-collar was pulled right up and his hat right down. I'd hardly have recognized him if he'd been my best friend.'

'You knew all about Tomson, at the drapery shop, of course, sir?'

'Never saw him in my life until I handed in that parcel. Had to remember where the shop was, as a matter of fact.'

'We've had our eye on him for some time. We think he may be a receiver of stolen goods.'

'I thought he might be, too, but it wasn't any business of mine. I simply collected the parcel and handed it over.'

'Thus carrying out the wishes of an unknown voice on the telephone . . . and in a public call-box at that?'

'I know it sounds silly, but it seemed a good idea at the time.'

'The gentlemen who get those kind of good ideas, sir, are apt to end up in trouble. Now, sir, I suggest that we are not being frank with one another. If I lay my cards on the table I shall expect to see *your* hand, too. I have reason to believe that you were bribed by Tomson to forget all about getting a receipt for Miss Faintley's parcel.'

'He gave me five pounds, and I took it. It wasn't as though I knew the first thing about Miss Faintley or where to contact her,' said Mandsell, giving way at last, 'but I did *not* take the money as a bribe. I shall pay it back.'

'Well, sir, as to that, we must take your word for it. But if you should decide to give us a little more information, well, I don't mind saying we could do with it. This is a funny kind of business, and those that help the authorities won't find reason to regret it. Could I have the name and address of your publishers, sir?'

'Certainly. Here's the letter they sent me, but, honestly, I can't help you. I certainly would if I could.'

'Many thanks, sir. You'll hear from us again in due course, when we've pushed the inquiry further forward.'

'Is that a threat, may I ask?'

'We don't threaten people, sir. But the law is the law, and the law is against murder, so, if you should remember anything else, sir – '

'There's nothing more to remember, and . . . well, I needn't have come to you, you know!'

'We quite appreciate that, sir, but murder's a very nasty business to be mixed up in.'

'Look here,' said Mandsell desperately, 'I don't know much about the law, but I've told the truth as far as I see it. Damn it all, I've even admitted now that I took the five pounds that miserable little tradesman offered me! All the same, it isn't my business if some wretched, unknown female chooses to get herself bumped off! I own to calling for the parcel. I didn't know then what was in it and I don't know now. It might have been a silly thing to do. I daresay it was. But I did it without thinking. I own, too, that I ought not to have accepted the five pounds, but I was desperate for money, turned out of my digs, and with no-where to go and nobody to turn to. I meant to pay back the money . . . I knew it was a fishy business . . . and I still mean to return it. I'm only waiting for my royalties to turn up. You've got no reason to keep badgering me like this!'

'Just one more question, and I'm through, sir, for the present. Can you be any more exact about the parcel?'

'I don't think so. It was about twenty inches long, twelve to fourteen inches wide, and, possibly, half an inch thick.'

'I see, sir. What about the weight? Could it have contained metal, for instance?'

'Good heavens, no. It was quite light. Could have been sent by post easily. Can't think why it wasn't. No reason at all for sending it by rail.'

'Thank you, sir. That may be very important. Now, if I may make a suggestion, I advise you to watch your step, same as it wouldn't have done Miss Faintley much harm if she had managed to watch hers a bit more closely. There's something funny going on, sir, and precautions may be very necessary. I'll go farther, and put you under police protection after this, if you like.'

'I can't imagine any danger. After all, I *did* hand over the parcel and Tomson knows it.'

'If he chooses to tell the real owners of the parcel that you didn't, you might be in quite a spot of trouble, sir. It wasn't very likely the parcel belonged to Miss Faintley. I have reason to think she was simply a sort of go-between. She didn't deliver the goods, so they bumped her off, but by this time Tomson will have wised-up the murderers that she never even saw this particular parcel, but that *you* – an unauthorized collector – did.'

'But that's tantamount to confessing he's kept it himself!'

'He's a foxy type, sir. He'll have thought of some yarn to fix the stealing on to *you*. He's let himself in so deep, it seems to me, that at present he's got far more reason (or so he thinks) to fear some crook than to fear the police. I could even bet on the sort of yarn he's told them. You came into the shop, he'll say, with the parcel, but wanted to stick him a good-sized sum for handing it over the counter. He refused your terms and pointed out it was Miss Faintley's business to pay you if she'd got you to do her job for her, and before he knew what was happening you shot out of the door and were up the street before he could say Jack Robinson. That's about the size of what he would tell these people, sir, and if Miss Faintley was murdered because they thought *she'd* kept the parcel . . . well, I hope you see what I mean, sir!'

Mandsell did see, but only in the sense that he saw violent actions on the films.

'All the same, they wouldn't dare touch me,' he said. He had that feeling, common to all healthy people, that troubles and violence come to others, but not to the onlooker. 'Still, if I note one of your Roberts tagging on to me, I'm to understand that his diligence is entirely on my behalf. Is that the ticket?'

'More or less, sir. But I hope you won't be aware of him. He won't be much good at his job if he's as obvious as all that.' He nodded genially, and went straight to Tomson's stores. No one was visible, so Darling shouted, 'Shop!' After a short interval Tomson came shuffling out from a room behind the counter.

'Ah, Tomson! Busy?'

'No, I ain't, not on a Monday.'

'Good. Back of the shop?'

'Yes, I suppose so. I'll hear the bell if anybody comes in, but Mondays is always slack.' Tomson sounded lugubrious. The flap of the counter came up and Darling passed through. The room behind the shop was dark and smelt of stale fish. Darling sat down at the table and Tomson took a rocking-chair at the side of the empty fireplace.

'This parcel for Miss Faintley. You knew what was in it, of course,' said the Inspector. 'Why don't you open up? There's nothing to connect you with the murder, and you could help us a lot if you liked.'

'Yes, and get myself jugged without the option. I know you nosey-parker coppers,' said Tomson morosely.

'Now, look here, Tomson, you've never been in trouble with us yet, so why begin? We know quite a lot about you, but we've never been able to prove anything – not for want of trying, let me tell you. But murder's an entirely different matter from the sort of thing you've been used to. And don't think I blame you, either, for trying to make a little bit on the side. It must be devilish difficult to make a living out of a small back-street business these days.'

'You're telling *me*! All right, then, here it is. I *do* take in parcels for one or two people, and I've been told to expect this parcel. I don't know what's in it, no more than you do, and that's gospel.'

'Oh? And hadn't you any idea of what was in *any* of the parcels you took in for Miss Faintley?'

'Sort of, of course. I mean to say, just common sense to find out what goes on. What I took in was statues and that.'

'Statues?'

'Yes, statues. Know what a statue is, don't you?' His self-confidence was returning.

'What sort of statues?' inquired Darling in a tone devoid of offence.

'Oh, nothing rude. Dancing girls and chaps in top-hats put on sideways. Once one got broke inside the parcel. That's 'ow I know, otherwise I wouldn't 'ave done. I wasn't paid to play nark to the police, I was paid to take in them parcels, and that's as far as it went.'

Darling smiled.

'Suppose I told you we have reason to think that the parcels contained diamonds from Amsterdam? Come on, out with it! Where are the diamonds now?'

'Easy on, now, Inspector!' Tomson's tone had changed. 'I've allowed a parcel got broke. It wasn't no fault of mine, and I never took no diamonds. Because why? – There wasn't no diamonds to take.'

'What happened to them, then? Don't tell me you were clever enough to piece the statue together again, so that the *real* consignee' – he paused, but Tomson did not help him – 'couldn't tell that it had ever been broken!'

'Of course not. I sent on the pieces and kept me mouth shut, but there wasn't no diamonds nor nothing in the parcel, and that I swear.'

'I'll *bet* you kept your mouth shut! What else did you keep?'

'Not diamonds, I swear it! I sent on the bits, like I said just now, so the other party didn't worry, I suppose. I said there'd been an accident with the thing. As a matter of fact, I felt properly had. There wasn't nothing but a leaf of fern.'

'Who is the other party?'

'I don't know. I never only write to box numbers.'

'What was the number of this particular box?'

'How d'you expect me to remember? It's news to me that it's again' the law to take parcels in to be called for!'

'Too right, I believe. Oh, by the way, were all the parcels alike?'

'Just exactly. Same shape, same weight, same size.'

'We have evidence that that isn't true. Don't try any funny stuff. What were the other parcels like?'

'I never took in no others.'

'Don't be a fool. Anyway, talking of the parcels you admit of accepting, how did the statues reach the end of their journey?'

'Collected up from this 'ere shop, of course.'

'By Miss Faintley?'

'She delivered 'em to me, but she never collected any up.'

'Well, who did, then?'

'I dunno.'

'How do you mean, you don't know?'

'All I done, I took in the parcels, see, and give a receipt. 'Ad to show the receipt to prove the package 'ad been 'anded over to my shop, I suppose. Well, when I gets the parcel, I writes to the box number, whatever it is – '

'How did you know which box number to write to? Was it a regular series?'

'No. I used to be given a different one each time.'

'By post? Did you get this information through the post?'

'That's right. Type-wrote, envelope and all, giving me the box number they was going to use next.'

'How often did the parcels come?'

'There wasn't no set time. Sometimes it 'ud be months, and once I 'ad three in a week.'

'How many altogether?'

The shopkeeper hesitated; then he handed over a small notebook.

'It's all in 'ere. You better stick to it. I been thinking, and I don't think I want to be mixed up in nothing like murder. Murder's wicked, that's what murder is.'

'Quite right, Tomson. And now, to go back to where we branched off, you say you don't know who collected the parcels from you. How was that?'

'Whoever it was 'ad a key to my shop-door. All I done was leave the parcel on the counter as soon as I'd wrote to the box number to say I'd got something for 'em, and then, next night, they'd come along with the key and let their-selves in and out, and take the parcel with 'em.'

'And you've no idea who came?'

'I wasn't paid to 'ave ideas, and the pay was reg'lar, whether any parcels come or not.'

'But you knew, with all this secrecy, that these people couldn't have been up to any good!'

'I thought they was on the windy side of the law, but it wasn't none of my business. And when I seen what there was . . . the bit of fern, I mean . . . in that statue, I didn't worry no more. A man's got to live, same as what you said yourself just now.'

'How did you first get into the game? Using this shop for letters that weren't to be delivered to private houses?'

'Could 'ave been, couldn't it? Your guess is as good as mine. It wasn't nothing wrong.'

'You're quite certain? . . . You wouldn't care to name any names?'

'I don't know no names, that's what. I've told you the truth because I don't want to get mixed up in no murders.'

'You haven't told me the whole truth, as I know for a fact. And don't bother to tell me you don't know who Mr Mandsell might be, because I'm sure you do, and, if you don't, you can guess.'

Tomson swore.

'I don't know what happened to it, I tell you!'

'Suit yourself, but, if you're going to be a fool and land yourself in a mess, don't come to us to get you out of it!'

Tomson laughed. His mirth had an unpleasant sound and Darling told him briefly to come off it.

'I don't want no police protection because I 'aven't done nothing wrong,' said Tomson, becoming plaintive. 'It's 'ard to make an honest living these days.'

'But not quite so hard to make a dishonest one,' retorted Darling. 'If you take my advice, you'll come clean. I'd much sooner believe Mr Mandsell's word than I would yours, for reasons we both understand, and Mr Mandsell's description of the parcels doesn't tally with yours. Now, then, what about it?'

But Tomson was either too wily, or too much afraid of his mysterious employers, to say more than:

'I can't 'elp what '*e* says, can I? I'm telling you what I know. It was statues and the one what got broke 'ad a bit of fern inside, and that's all.'

Darling returned to Vardon.

'It's still all guesswork what the parcels contained,' he said. 'Either Tomson's lying, or else there are two types of parcels. Our best plan, at this end, is to keep an eye on this chap Mandsell, I think. There's a gang at work, of course. That sticks out a mile. If the gang try and lay Mandsell out we ought to get *them*, and if he tries to contact them we ought to get *him*.'

'Do you think he was in with Miss Faintley, then, and his story about the other fellow who came out of the telephone box is all lies?'

'No, I'm inclined to believe him, but it doesn't hurt to keep an open mind. Anything doing at *your* end?'

'Nothing at all, so far. We've established (to our own satisfaction, anyway) that the house on the cliffs outside which the body was found was not being lived in. One room seems to have been visited occasionally, but even that hasn't got a bed in it, and there are no arrangements for cooking except a kitchen range which obviously hasn't been used for years.'

'Fingerprints?'

'What do *you* think? And yet the place is thick with dust! No, we're not looking for a cosh-boy or a jealous lover. I agree with you that we're looking for a gang, and those parcels are at the root of the matter. I don't suppose it would help much, but for the sake of curiosity I'd like to know whether Tomson *is* lying about the parcel he says was broken. Mandsell swears his was a flat one, and not heavy, so that doesn't sound like counterfeit coins or diamonds. It could be counterfeit notes, though. We ought to go to Hagford Junction next to see the parcels clerk. If he's been in the habit of handing parcels over to Miss Faintley it shouldn't tax his memory too much to remember what they were like.'

'Yes, we must check on that clerk.' They motored at once to the station. Here they met with a slight check. The man was on leave, and nobody knew his holiday address. The railway station staff were positive, however, that he had gone away. He had shown them folders describing coach tours and had made it clear that he was going to book one for himself and his brother. The brother nobody had met. The name was Price.

Darling took down the address he was given and went to the house, but nobody answered his knock, and a neighbour came out and said that she had seen the brothers go off with suitcases. So that was that for a bit, thought Darling. He decided that it did not matter very much. When however, at the end of the following week he returned to the station without Vardon, who had gone back to Torbury, it was to learn that the Left Luggage clerk had not returned to duty at the appointed time, and that no explanation was forthcoming of his absence.

'So it looks as though he might have been mixed up in it at least as much as Tomson is,' Darling confided to Vardon when next they met. 'I daresay he's only one of the smaller fry ... certainly nobody would trust *Tomson* very far! ...

but I'd like to have got my hooks on him, especially now I know he's vamoosed.'

'Stymie! The inquest'll have to be resumed some time or other, but we can't add any more evidence at present. Can you tackle the older Miss Faintley again, and see if she can cough up any more?'

'I can try, but, although she's a spiteful, dissatisfied old besom, I think she's told us everything she knows.'

'Yes, I was afraid perhaps she had.'

'I'll try her, anyway. In fact, I'm going to get a warrant and search the flat.'

'She won't like that, but it ought to be done. And you can't get Tomson to squeal?'

'I've a hunch he's in the same boat as Miss Faintley was, and if it *is* a gang we're after, they wouldn't give a little rat like him very much to squeal about, or else not much time to do the squealing. Have to get a description of that Left Luggage clerk. He'll have to be found, although I wouldn't mind betting that his disappearance has nothing to do with the parcels or the murder.'

'Pity petty cash was ever invented,' said Vardon. 'How would it be if we got two independent descriptions of the fellow, one from the station people and the other from Mandsell? Might act as a useful check on Mandsell, don't you think?'

'You mean that if Mandsell *is* concerned in the business (I don't believe it, you know!) his description of the clerk is likely to be misleading? Right. Let's try it. The station people first, of course. Then we can measure up what they say against anything Mandsell may tell us.'

The description of the missing man would fit a good many people, the two police officers decided. There was only one helpful point. He had been left-handed to such an extent that it amounted to a physical idiosyncrasy of a very definite kind. It seemed as though his right hand was almost useless. Even the heaviest parcels on his shelves he would attempt to take down or put up using his left hand only. Otherwise, he was a brown-haired man of thirty-five or so, of medium height, slim without being noticeably thin, brown-eyed, with a mole on the right cheek-bone.

The officers checked this information with his landlady, who confirmed it, and said that when the brothers left their lodgings for their holiday, each had been wearing grey flannel trousers, a white open-neck shirt, Mr Tavy Price (the railway clerk) a green-fawn sports jacket, Mr Hugh Price a brown one. Their suitcases were of dark-brown fibre and had been labelled *Mohawk Tours*.

Mandsell's description tallied exactly with that given by the station officials. Without being prompted, he even commented upon the extreme left-handedness of the luggage clerk.

'It was almost like a deformity,' he said, 'but he seemed to manage all right.'

The two police officers had obtained from the landlady the address of the Price brothers' doctor. He could offer no explanation of the awkward and noticeable left-handedness, but thought it was probably due to an obstinate reaction from having had to be right-handed at school. In spite of modern ideas upon the subject, he declared, some teachers were still wicked and misguided enough to try to force left-handed boys to use the right hand for writing and carpentry and so forth. He held forth upon the iniquity of this practice, added that there was nothing physically wrong with Price's right hand and arm, and left the officers little the wiser.

'I'd better get on to *Mohawk Tours*,' said Darling. 'Not that they'll be able to help much. If they'd lost a cash customer *en route* they'd have reported it before this. Still, I must see them.'

'Right. I must get back to Torbury. You'll let me know anything useful?'

'Of course, and that goes for you, too.'

The two detective-inspectors parted on terms of personal goodwill and official disappointment that the inquiry was not bearing much fruit, and Darling went straight to the local office which booked places on *Mohawk Tours* motor-coaches. As he walked along the High Street at Hagford, another point occurred to him. As Price was employed by the railway, he would be allowed some travel concessions. It seemed odd that he should forego these on his annual holiday. However, probably he merely wanted a change.

Mohawk Tours were helpful – almost too helpful, in fact. Two men named Price had indeed taken their tour, and had been very popular with the party. Darling, who could never have been accused of scamping his job, asked whether one of them had not been very noticeably left-handed.

'I could not say, but the driver who took out that tour may be having his change-over day. I will ring up,' said the agency clerk, who was curious to know what this was all about. The result of his inquiry was interesting. Both Prices had played cards with the driver, who was also the courier. Both were slick dealers. Both dealt right-handed and at lightning speed. He had never noticed either of them to be left-handed at table or elsewhere.

A description of the brothers, sought eagerly now by the Inspector, did not tally in the slightest with the description given by the landlady, the station staff, or Mandsell, all of whom had been in agreement.

'So what's happened to the Prices is anybody's guess,' said Darling on the telephone to Vardon. 'We're getting on their trail at once. Someone impersonated them on that trip, but whether it was a put-up job, or whether they've been kidnapped, it's hard to say. Anything more from your end?'

'Nothing yet, and Mrs Bradley and her secretary are coming your way, I think. The old lady, between ourselves, is as much at sea as the rest of us, I fancy. Still, we've got our orders to give her all the gen, so I'll pass on what you've told me. What about the Faintley aunt and the search warrant?'

'I haven't applied for one yet. I may not need to. My own view is that Faintley was merely a stooge – someone obviously respectable, who could be trusted to pick up the parcels.'

'What do *you* think they contained? – dynamite?'

'Snow. That's my guess up to date. Snow in the statues and instructions in the flat package collected by Mandsell.'

'No wonder Tomson's scared. I've been thinking along those lines myself, as a matter of fact, but would Tomson have invented anything so unlikely as *ferns* being hidden in the statues?'

'No. It's a code word, I expect. He hopes to diddle us with it, and, up to date, he's succeeded. He's monkey-clever, you know. We've had him on our books for years, and have never caught him out yet. I'm hoping he's stubbed his toe this time, though.'

CHAPTER SIX

MYSTERY MEN

*

'When I burned in desire to question them further,
they made themselves air, into which they vanished.'

SHAKESPEARE – *Macbeth*

'DEAR me,' said Mrs Bradley, meeting Mark at the entrance to the dining-room, 'and what does this betoken?'

'We've finished breakfast,' replied Mark, 'and we're going home to-day.' He glanced down at his best trousers. 'Everything's packed, and we're going out for a bit of a walk before lunch, and then, directly lunch is over, we shall be off. I shan't be sorry.'

'I, too, have had my fill of Cromlech,' Mrs Bradley agreed. 'A pleasing village, but, on the whole, rather lacking in amenities.'

'Saw it all the first day,' muttered Mark. 'There's nothing decent to do except bathe, and the tide isn't always right for that, and if you take a boat out you've got to have a boatman. Now, if I'd gone to France . . .' He proceeded to give a colourful description of the delights which he and Ellison had envisaged.

'France,' said Mrs Bradley reminiscently. 'Ah, yes, so you told me before. I shall fly to Lascaux to-morrow . . . at least, not all the way to Lascaux, but to the airport nearest to it.'

'To-morrow? Oh, I say, you *are* lucky!'

'When does school reopen?'

'Wednesday, worse luck. Still, I shall see Ellison again. They've gone to Jersey.'

'Indeed? Well, you had better solicit your dear parents'

permission to come with me to France. It will not be a long
visit because neither of us can spare the time, but we could
be back by Monday evening.'

'I *say!*' shouted Mark. 'Do you mean it?' He rushed off
at once, and brought his father back with him. The parental
blessing was evoked, and the Torbury aerodrome hopped
one calm, one excited and one puzzled passenger to
Northolt. There a specially commissioned police car rushed
them to Heath Row.

'But I can't see what all this is in aid of,' said Laura
plaintively to the driver, who happened to be her fiancé,
Detective-Inspector Gavin of Scotland Yard. 'What's
cooking?'

'Mrs Croc. did not confide in us. She said she was tired of
the Faintley case. *We're* not in on it officially, but off the
record we've made a few inquiries about the Faintleys, as
they used to live in London –'

'Anything interesting about them?'

'Damn-all. Just an ordinary suburban family respected if
not loved. Bombed out in 1941. Pop was a shop steward,
daughter trained as a teacher. Otherwise, as we say in our
patois, nothing known.'

'What do *you* make of it?'

'I'd have said cosh and grab, but the fact that the handbag and that expensive watch were left behind by the
murderer effectively disposes of *that* theory, and there was
no attempt at funny business, according to the medical
evidence at the first inquest . . . just the one clean thrust of
the Commando knife. The chap was no bungler, I'll say
that for him. He just took a dislike to her, apparently, and
she'd had it. I wish we knew why. I imagine your boss has
rumbled something, but she's not likely to tell us what it is
until she's pretty sure. Where's she actually making for?'

'Lascaux. The caves, you know.'

'Oh, ah? Tells us a lot, doesn't it? Still, we've got standing orders from the high-ups to afford her any facilities she
wants, and apparently she wants Air France, and here we
are!'

'I've decided to leave you to your own devices for a few days, dear Laura,' said Mrs Bradley, as they stood waiting for the aeroplane. 'Don't get into mischief. Remember that I place a high value upon your services. Oh, and our good Gavin, who has acquired a short term of leave of absence, may occupy my room at Cromlech while I'm away.'

'He can't. He's going to drive me back to-night and stay the night, and then I'm pushing him off to Scotland to visit his mother. I can't have him around while I'm so busy.'

'Well, be reasonable in carrying out your plans. I realize that nothing will keep you away from that cliff-top house where you found the body. Now that the police have concluded their investigations there, I have an instinctive feeling –'

'You're right, at that. I *did* think of infesting the place again when I get back. I don't suppose there's a thing to find out, and, even though the police pretend to have given up crawling all over it, I daresay some of them have been told to check the visitors. One thing, it's such a brute of a climb to get in the only way one can ... because they're sure to have filled up that gap that young Mark and I made with our battering ram ... that I don't suppose many people will trouble themselves to go there, especially as the exact locality hasn't been made too public.'

'Well, I do not propose to fuss, but I would like to point out that the house may have *been* empty the last time you went there, or it may only have *seemed* empty. It is possible that you might be recognized.'

'And you think it won't be healthy up there for snoopers? I know. I'll look out for myself, so you need not worry.'

'I have no intention of worrying, child. Good luck to your hunting. Not that I think there will be very much to find out.'

Laura was greatly attached to her boat, the *Canto Five,* and spent half an hour or so in messing about checking petrol, oil, stores, and the engine before she took in her anchor, so that it was a quarter to three on the following afternoon before she got away from her anchorage. Her scheme was twofold. She had a desire to see the picturesque little village of Wedlock, which lay about two miles in from the coast, and she also had a theory that, once she had rounded the tremendous headland on which the mystery house was built, it might be possible to find a way up to the house without the fatiguing climb which had taken her and Mark to the house when she had discovered Miss Faintley's body. There must, she argued, be an easier way up than either of the paths they had used. Fuel and provisions had had to be taken to the place when it was used as a school. Therefore there must be a road.

It was pleasant cruising weather. She put out to sea and gave the rocky headland a wide berth. Then as she came round the great bend, she began to edge in towards the shore. As she had expected from her study of map and chart, the headland sloped down on the north-east side to a sandy bay. She made for the middle of this, felt her way in, and, at three fathoms, paid out plenty of chain to hold on the sandy bottom, took to the dinghy and rowed herself ashore. She beached the little boat well up on an incoming tide, and took careful stock of her surroundings.

There were a good many people on the beach, and there was another cabin cruiser anchored some distance off, too far away for Laura to be able to take stock of it. A low sea-wall bounded the sand, and, from it, a steep road, possible, however, for cars, went up from the sea towards some pleasantly-situated houses. Half-way up this road another branched off at right-angles and was marked: *Cromlech Down School Only. Private.*

'This is it,' thought Laura. Firmly grasping the ash-plant which she had brought with her in the dinghy, she began to ascend the slope. The surface was good, and a series of serpentine windings kept the gradients at about (she judged) one in nine. The bends made the walk a long one, and she decided that she must have covered the better part of six miles before she came in sight of the house she was looking for. On this side it was fenced in with iron palings in which

were set the main double gates. A derelict lodge, with
vacant windows and part of the roof off, flanked these and
had obviously been unoccupied for years, but the gates,
although they were locked, offered no obstacle to the tall
and agile Laura. She put her ash-plant between the bars and
then climbed over, aware that, if anyone happened to be
looking out, she was in full view from the house. She picked
up her stick and sauntered forward.

The gardens, if such they could be called, were, like the
part of them that she and Mark had already seen, very
much neglected. She perambulated unkempt paths, keeping
the house in view but circumnavigating it, until she came
round to the side where she had made entrance to find the
body. There was the straight path which, when she had seen
it last, had been carefully smoothed and sanded. It was
much trampled now, probably, she thought, by policemen's
boots. She wondered whether the police had discovered any
clues to the identity of Miss Faintley's assailant, and she
left the path to inspect the bush beneath which Miss
Faintley's head had been thrust. It was likely that the
woman had been struck down on the path, and then the
path resanded to obscure footprints and perhaps to cover
up blood. The painstaking police no doubt had swept the
path, taken a sample, and put the sand back.

She turned away, walked back to the path and followed
it up to the house. At the great front door she knocked. The
reverberation of emptiness came booming at her. She
listened intently, but, once the sound of her own knocking
had died, the silence, except for screaming gulls whom the
noise, most likely, had disturbed, and the far-off sound of
the sea on the headland rocks, settled down again even as,
after a minute or two, the gulls returned to their fastnesses,
the ledges and clefts of the cliff.

Laura went on round the house and found the window
which (presumably) the police had broken in order to force
an entrance. The catch was temptingly exposed. Laura was
not the person to ignore a challenge. She pushed back the
catch, opened the window and inserted her head. In a very

loud voice she called out: 'Hullo, there! Anybody in?'

There was no answer. A sudden breeze blew past her ear and shut an open door with a bang which sounded loud enough to bring down the house.

'Hope it hasn't jammed!' thought Laura. She waited for a few moments to see whether the slam of the door would bring anybody to find out what had happened, but everything remained still, so she climbed in through the window, determined to tour the house.

It was a big place. Besides the kitchen regions and a large, much-scrawled-upon room which seemed to speak of bored children on wet afternoons and which was completely unfurnished even to the bare floorboards much trampled, again, she supposed, by policemen, there were seven other rooms on the ground floor. Only one of these, the curtained room she had seen on her first visit, was furnished. It contained a carpet, a suite of upholstered furniture, several small chairs, a large table (much scratched), a rusty metal filing-cabinet which she opened and found to be empty, and a case of pressed ferns. This was fastened to the wall and each exhibit was labelled, both botanically and in English, thus:*

Polypodium Vulgare	Common Polypody
Polystichum Lonchitis	Holly Fern
Trichomanes Radicans	British Fern
Asplenium Ceterach	Scaly Spleenwort
Asplenium Septentrionale	Forked Spleenwort
Lastrea Filix-Mas	Male Fern
Polypodium Phegopteris	Beech Fern
Asplenium Fontanum	Smooth-Rock Spleenwort
Asplenium Marinum	Sea Spleenwort
Athyrium Filix-Foemina	Lady Fern
Botrychium Lunaria	Moonwort
Blechnum Spicant	Hard Fern
Lastreas (Nephrodium)	Buckler Fern
Ophioglossum Vulgatum	Adder's-Tongue Fern
Osmunda Regalis	Royal Fern

*The author is indebted to C. T. Druery's book *British Ferns and their Varieties*, kindly lent by Miss Ella Vinall, for this information.

'Shades of the prison house!' said Laura aloud, thinking of her own schooldays. 'Wonder why they didn't take it with them?' The specimens were indeed remarkably well preserved and had been carefully – one would say lovingly – mounted, and the printing, carried out in Indian ink, was both artistic and neat. The other downstairs rooms having provided nothing of interest, Laura decided to try the rooms on the first floor. These did not coincide in every case with the ground floor rooms, and she concluded that some had been considerably altered, possibly to provide dormitories. This theory was substantiated by her discovery of a row of small washbasins, five tiny bathrooms with partitions between them which did not reach the ceiling, and, opposite them, a row of water-closets.

There was a third storey to the house but this yielded nothing of the slightest interest; neither did two attics at the top of a small wooden staircase. Bored by her fruitless exploration, Laura went to one of the attic windows. It was heavily cobwebbed, and she was about to brush aside some of this obscurity to look out upon the view when she drew back. The attic window overlooked the part of the garden between the house and the ruined lodge, and two men were approaching.

'Holiday sightseers,' was her first impression. 'Wonder whether they've come to see the spot marked X or not? I didn't know the news was all that much public.'

She knelt on the boarded floor and did her best to peer through the window without getting too near the glass. But the men were no casual holiday-makers in spite of their hatlessness and careless holiday clothes. They came straight up to the house and one of them thundered on the door just as she had done, but even louder.

She crept to the top of the attic staircase and prayed that no creaking board would betray her, for, after a very short interval, the men let themselves in. She could hear their voices in the hall. Then they went into one of the rooms. She heard the door being shut.

Clutching her ash-plant, she began to creep down the

stairs. They could hardly be Miss Faintley's murderers, she
decided, to come boldly and in broad daylight like this, but
they obviously had some right to be in the house, which she
most certainly had not. It would entail no end of awkward
explanation if she were caught on the premises. They might
even be police officers, although she did not think that
plain-clothes men would wear cricket shirts, sweaters and
grey flannel bags. Whoever they were, it behoved her to
get away as circumspectly and as quickly as she could.

There was no sound of voices when she came to the foot
of the staircase. She knew which room the men were in
because it was the only one in which the door was shut. She
herself had been careful to leave all the inside doors open
as she had found them. Taking special care, and thankful
that she was still wearing the rubber-soled shoes she used
on the boat, she made her way to the kitchen and climbed
out of the open window. She did not attempt to close it. The
men, if they investigated, must think that it had been left as
it was by the police.

Keeping on the grass, she made for the bushes, and,
stooping very low, crept round them until she was out of
line with the windows behind which lurked the two
mysterious visitors. As she went, she pondered. The men
had obviously been furnished with a key to the front door.
Why, then, she wondered, had they troubled to beat that
thunderous tattoo? The only explanation was that they had
tried to find out, just as she had, whether the house was
inhabited. But if they had the right to enter, and were
furnished with the means of entry, why did they need to
find out whether the house was occupied or empty? Did
they expect that the police were still in possession?

As there seemed to be no obvious answer to this question
she decided to wait in hiding for a bit and find out whether
there was anything more to be learnt. The one furnished
room intrigued her. As there was no bed, it did not seem
likely that it had been a caretaker's lodging. Still thinking
deeply, she reached the crumbling lodge. It seemed to offer
as good a bit of cover as anywhere else, and, although the

roof was damaged, it certainly offered some prospect of shelter from the storm which was obviously gathering, for the sky had become overcast and already a few spots of heavy summer rain were splashing down on her head.

The floors of the lodge had disappeared. The interior was rank with nettles and bright with patches of willowherb. Laura, in her seafaring slacks, was able to cope with the nettles. She waded through them to shelter and settled down to keep watch from one of the broken windows which looked towards the house. She did not need to wait long. At the end of about a quarter of an hour the men appeared. By this time it was pouring with rain, and, to her great disappointment, both men were wearing large bandana handkerchiefs which partly obscured their faces.

'Shades of Jesse James!' thought Laura, vexed. 'Now I shall never be able to recognize them if ever I meet them again! What a nuisance that attic window was all cob-webs!' Their heads, too, were bent against the wind which was blowing full in their faces, and this made any chance of memorizing their appearance even more difficult. To her great interest, however, they were carrying a large package draped in one of the curtains which had been up at the windows of the room which they had entered.

Laura gave them another quarter of an hour. Then she went back to the house, climbed in, and went straight to the furnished room to try to identify their burden. This was easy enough. Where the case of ferns had been was an empty wall with only the plug-marks showing.

'Curiouser and curiouser,' thought Laura. 'What on earth can they want with that?'

She left the house at once . . . by the front door, this time . . . and trotted back to the lodge. Here she climbed the gate and ran down the winding slope to the shore. She had no fear of catching up with the men and so betraying that she had been to the house. They had more than twenty minutes' start of her and had been walking as fast as the wind and their burden would allow.

Neither was there any sign of them on the beach. Moreover

the other cruiser had gone. There might be no significance in this, as there was no evidence that the two men had come from the cruiser. It might have belonged to anyone. Laura returned in her own boat to Cromlech, and remembered, too late, that she had not been to the village of Wedlock after all. Next day she reported to Vardon that the case of ferns had been carried away from the house, and gave what description she could of the two men.

'Fit hundreds of people,' said Vardon. 'Still, you *might* be able to pick them out again if you saw them.'

Laura thought this very unlikely, and could see that he did, too. She half expected a reprimand for going alone to the house, but this did not come.

'Funny about the ferns,' she said, hoping for information.

'Funny case altogether, Miss Menzies. What's Mrs Bradley up to? We heard she was going to France.'

'She's gone. I don't know what the idea is. We'll know more when she comes back. She's taken young Mark Street along with her. I expect them back on Monday night.'

'I see. Your two men might interest Detective-Inspector Darling. He's lost a couple of rather interesting brothers!'

To Mark the whole of the journey was a fairy-tale told for his benefit. When at last they reached the caves Mrs Bradley put him in charge of a guide and went on her own tour of inspection. It was not her presence that Mark needed. Contrary to her satellites' impression that she had received a kind of spirit message that Lascaux would provide the solution of their problem, or even the most faint, elusive clue that Miss Faintley's mysterious activities and the riddle of her death were in some way connected with the prehistoric art of the caves, she had acted merely in obedience to one of her strongest emotions, a deep, abiding, amused and tender love of small boys. Mark, she sensed, had been much more bitterly resentful of and disappointed at the failure of his plan to visit France than his parents realized. Resentfulness and disappointment, she was well aware, do not strengthen character at Mark's age; she

considered it doubtful whether they did at any age. The
Faintley case would make no further progress, she surmised,
until school reopened and Miss Faintley's life could be
regarded from another angle. The opportunity was present,
therefore, to remove the poison from Mark's mind. True,
she was not the no-doubt gallant and resourceful Ellison,
but perhaps to fly to France instead of going by sea and
train would compensate somewhat for that.

That it had more than compensated she was soon aware,
and the boy's silent ecstasy enhanced her own pleasure in
the trip. The custodians of Lascaux knew her, for she had
spent several months there researching into the psycho-
logical significance of the Aurignacian cave-decorations and
in attempting to read their symbolism in the light of modern
psycho-analytical knowledge, so they allowed her to wander
at will while she sought out her own favourite paintings,
including that of the so-called Apocalyptic Beast with his
forward-pointing horns, his watchful head, and his attitude
of alertness, his firm legs planted and yet a-quiver, like
those of a hunter's hound. There was nothing dog-like,
however, about this sagging-bellied, demoniacal creature
with the Indian bullock's bulge on his shoulders and his
tremendously-muscled thighs. He was master, not servant,
in the cave.

When she rejoined Mark she had a short talk with the
guide, and obtained an item of intelligence which she filed
in her mind as being too good to be true. She had guessed
that the prehistoric caves, not Lascaux, particularly, but
many of those which could be found all along the Dordogne,
had been used during the war by the French Resistance.
What she learned now was that a man called Bannister had
taken a prominent part in the Resistance, having been, in
fact, a British Intelligence officer. The name stuck. Mark,
who had almost no French, picked it up, too.

'He said Monsieur Bannistaire,' he remarked. 'Didn't
mean Mr Bannister, did he?'

'I dare not suppose that he meant *your* Mr Bannister,
child.'

'Well, Bannister's been here, to Lascaux. It wasn't just that he'd bought the book. I mean, you could tell, just like when they give you a jogger lesson on some place either they've been to or they haven't. You can always tell. Besides, why should a maths beak tell us about a thing like this unless he'd been here?'

'Sound arguments, logically expressed, child.'

'But why *caves?*' demanded Laura when they got back.

'Ferns might grow in them,' Mrs Bradley cryptically replied. 'From what I hear from our indefatigable police officers, ferns would appear to be the foliage, if not entirely the root, of the matter.'

CHAPTER SEVEN

MISS GOLIGHTLY

*

'Stern Pluto shall himself to mirth betake,
And crownéd ghosts shall banquet for thy sake.'

SHAKERLEY MARMION – *Proserpine*

LAURA knew her employer far too well to ask too many questions, but she turned over Mrs Bradley's remark about caves and ferns, and light dawned.

'You went inside that house yourself with the police, and spotted that case of ferns,' she said at breakfast next morning. Mrs Bradley cackled at, but did not deny, this statement.

'We must bring our holiday to a close,' she remarked. 'There are various people we ought to see and various things we ought to do before we come back to Cromlech.'

'We *are* coming back, then? I rather hoped we were. We've had less intriguing cases than this one. Ferns!' She brooded, visualizing them growing. There was an old lady in her home town who kept the front-room window full of them to make a screen so that she could peer out but the passers-by could not peer in. There were harts-tongue ferns, shining in the Devonshire rain; ferns under dripping cascades in the north from which Laura came; ferns in damp woods; bracken fronds (not, she supposed, true ferns) in the New Forest clearings, on the sandy wastes around Sandringham, all over Surrey and Exmoor. The road from Porlock to Lynmouth was bordered with them. There were rare varieties of ferns much prized by collectors. There was maidenhair fern for bouquets or to put with carnations to make a spray for a dance frock. But all these ferns were living. They began in their infancy wrapped round by, curled up in, a sort of red-brown moss. They unfolded, prettiest before they reached maturity. They ate and drank and breathed and propagated their kind. There had been ferns before there were monkeys or men. There were ferns so tiny that only a botanist would find them; and there were ferns like trees – ferns as tall and as graceful as palms.

She found herself disliking ferns very much.

'They're sinister, aren't they?' she said aloud. Mrs Bradley cackled again, but did not answer the question. Instead she observed:

'A letter from the Queen to play croquet.'

'The Duchess in this case being –?'

'Mark's headmistress.'

'Why her? . . . Oh, of course! The late Faintley's boss. Don't suppose she knows very much about her.'

'We must leave no stone unturned –'

'No avenue unexplored. Right-o. Are you coming back with me in the cruiser, or would you prefer to go by train? The weather's cleared up again, thank goodness, so it ought to be quite a decent trip. To think, if it hadn't been for that beastly rain, I could have got those two men identified! I'm sure they were up to no good.'

'I always enjoy a sea-trip,' said Mrs Bradley. 'What a pity the boy's mother was too nervous to allow him to join us! And don't worry too much about the men. You certainly did everything you could, and even if you *had* seen their faces it is most unlikely that it would have helped.'

'I suppose,' suggested Laura, 'it wouldn't be a good idea to push along to that house again and have another look round?'

'I hardly think so, child. The men have got what they wanted. They are not likely to take the risk of turning up there again, and you saw for yourself how little the house has to tell us. Until the men proved its value by removing it, there was nothing to suggest that the case of ferns had any significance. Now we know it has, and I am infinitely obliged to you for finding that out.'

'You'd have found it out for yourself, later on,' said Laura shrewdly. 'I still don't believe you flew to France just to find smugglers' caves.'

'Those were not smugglers' caves, child, but I will admit that after I had been over that house (as you surmised) with the police, I had a long conversation over the telephone with the last known occupant of the house. I asked him what he had left behind, because it seemed inexplicable that he should have left one room more or less furnished.'

'How did you get in touch with him?'

'The police knew his name, of course, as the school had been advertised in all the local papers for miles around, and a scholastic agency soon put me upon his track. He replied that nothing had been left behind, so far as he remembered. Then I mentioned the case of ferns, but he was certain that the school had never possessed one. Interesting, is it not?'

'Focus on ferns, as the B.B.C. would say. But why France? We deduced you must have got hold of some information, or else had the whale of a hunch.'

'I thought Mark would like the trip, child.'

Laura looked at her suspiciously.

'Now stop pulling my leg,' she said, 'and come and help me overhaul the gear.'

'No. You go and see to the boat. I'll pack,' her employer replied. 'We must be off betimes in the morning.'

'For me as well? You're an angel. Celestine packed for me coming down. If she hadn't I should have brought about half the things I did bring. I can't think how she gets what she does into a suitcase. A cabin trunk wouldn't contain it all if *I* did the packing!'

It was not a long run from Cromlech to the Hamble River, and the early morning was ideal. The cruiser bounced and nose-dived, flung up spray, and spread a fantail of foaming wash behind her. It was an exhilarating trip. It also seemed a long way from the magic caves of Lascaux, Mrs Bradley reflected – about forty thousand years, in fact.

'There we are,' said Laura, when she had brought the cruiser over from the Calshott side in order to get a good view of the buoy which marked the river entrance. She altered course from due north to north-east to follow the channel. It was not a tricky entrance, particularly on such a good day, but Mrs Bradley remained seated and silent whilst Laura performed the necessary manoeuvres, for the river was popular with yachtsmen who had to be given right of way, and, at that time of year, it was crowded.

Skilful and careful, Laura came on past Warsash and Bursledon, and at last brought the *Canto Five* to her usual moorings.

'There's George with the car,' she said when the cruiser was tied up. 'Good. He can help with the luggage.'

The stocky chauffeur saluted them gravely, tucked them into the back seat, stowed away the suitcases and said, 'The Lyndhurst road, madam?'

'Yes, George. We want our lunch. Do you know where Kindleford is?'

'I have heard of it, madam. I will look it up on the map. The papers have made an interesting thing of the case of Miss Lilian Faintley.'

'Was her name Lilian? Oh, yes, I remember it was Lilian at the inquest. Are you acquainted with any headmistresses, George?'

'Only with one, madam, and she, unfortunately, is no longer among us.'

'Indeed? And who was that?'

'The lady who directed my infant intelligence from the age of five until seven, madam. I had an immense passion for her. I may say, without offence, that, apart from my mother, she is the only woman I have ever really loved.'

'Present company excepted,' said Laura, with a mischievous grin.

'Naturally, miss,' agreed the chauffeur with unimpaired gravity.

'I've never taken the micky out of George yet,' said Laura regretfully, as they drove off towards the green tunnels and sunny heaths of the New Forest. 'Do you suppose he ever laughs?'

'I have known him to do so once, many years ago, when a man laying down the law to him on the subject of types of cars, slipped and fell backwards into a tub of swill.'

'I'd like to have been there. When do we pursue this headmistress at Kindleford school?'

'Mark tells me that the school reopens on Wednesday – that is, to-morrow – so there is little doubt that Miss Golightly will be there preparing for the new school year, and we should be able to obtain a comparatively uninterrupted interview with her if we set off directly after lunch.'

'She *will* bless us! Still, that can't be helped. What part, if any, do I play?'

'Time will show, child. Look! Quite a number of New Forest ponies! I owned one when I was a child.'

Laura glanced at her. She found this sudden change of subject disquieting. She said, 'Did you?' in a non-committal voice and changed the subject herself.

'Are you going to the Kindleford police, as well as to Miss Golightly?'

'Yes, I am. Some interesting news came through from them to the Inspector who is investigating the death at Cromlech. It seems that a certain Mr Mandsell, an impecunious author –'

'Aren't they all?'

'I imagine so ... went to the Kindleford police as soon as he read about the murder, and told them a rather interesting story which may have considerable significance. It appears that this Mr Mandsell took, on a public telephone, a call from Miss Faintley which, it had clearly been arranged, was to have been picked up by somebody else. The result was that Mr Mandsell, for a whim, went to a railway station, picked up a parcel and delivered it at an obscure and not too much above-board little shop in a back street. He had been told to ask for a receipt, forgot to do so, went back and was blandly informed that no parcel had been handed in.'

'Very fishy. Whom did Miss Faintley think she'd been talking to on the phone? Did that come out?'

'No, it did not, and the police have no clue to his identity. But for Mr Mandsell's having picked up the call by mistake, they would not even know that this man existed.'

'Mandsell may be lying?'

'The Kindleford police do not think so. They have made inquiries, and there is no reason to doubt that he had never so much as heard of Miss Faintley before. My own view, from what little I know at present, is that Miss Faintley's correspondent was one of the men teachers at the school.'

'A teacher? What makes you think that? Teachers, on the whole, are not given to mixing themselves up with fishy parcels and grimy, two-purpose little shops, are they?'

'No, decidedly they are not, but one or two things in Mr Mandsell's evidence struck me as pointers to Miss Faintley's collaborator. First, although there was this arrangement to call some man up on a public telephone at a given time –'

'You'd think it would have been more practical for *him* to have called *her* up, under those circumstances, wouldn't you?'

'You certainly would ... but I'm coming to that. It all fits in with my theory that he was a teacher. Well, now: Miss Faintley lived with an aunt in this little provincial town of Kindleford, but we know from the police that the aunt's house is not on the telephone. Therefore, wherever she was, Miss Faintley was not at home when she spoke to Mandsell. The time, incidentally, was round about nine in the evening. All the shops, including the post office, were shut, and had been, all the afternoon.'

'Yes, she must have been at school,' said Laura, 'but wasn't it rather late in the evening for that?'

'It was the end of the term, remember. It is likely that some festivity was going on ...a tennis dance, perhaps. It is a mixed school with a mixed staff, you see.'

'Oh, yes. And that would account for her having never

known when she was likely to be interrupted on the telephone, I suppose.'

'Then, there were references to people being about in the
vestibule.'

'Yes, that does, perhaps, sound rather schooly. Oh, but,
look here, if you're right, it ought to be easy enough to find
out who her correspondent was supposed to have been! If
there was a dance on, or some other school function, you'd
only have to check with the staff to find out which master
wasn't present. I mean, whoever he is, he must know by
now that Miss Faintley was murdered, and he must be
guilty of the murder, I should say, or he'd have come
forward by this time.'

'That last is not a warrantable assumption. He may be
abroad for his holiday and, if so, he may not have seen
the London papers. But you are right to suggest that we
may be able to discover his identity by checking whether
he was present or not at the school on that particular evening.'

'Of course, he may not be one of the masters. I still think
that.'

'I think he is. If Mr Mandsell reported the conversation
correctly, the woman's voice told him that it was Faintley
speaking. He, quite naturally, thought she was using the
adverb "faintly" and assured her that her voice was not
faint! But you see what the implication is?'

'Just giving her surname, you mean? Yes, most women
put Miss or Mrs in front if they don't give their Christian
name, don't they?'

'Yes, that is the whole point! She did not put anything
in front of her surname until he misunderstood, therefore
it is almost certain that she was talking to someone to
whom habitually she was known as Faintley, and not as
Miss Faintley. That surely suggests a colleague. The only
other kind of person who calls women by their surname is
the employer of a domestic servant, and that, in the case
of Miss Faintley, would scarcely apply – '

'Unless the parcel was part of a dark and criminal deed,

and Miss Faintley was, although not a domestic, definitely the servant of the man she thought she was speaking to.'

'Quite true, but the school is the likeliest and certainly the easiest starting-point for our investigations in Kindleford, and Miss Golightly is the person to tackle. As I say, she is almost certain to be on the premises, for there is always much to be done when the school year opens.'

'It's bound to be a nasty sort of place,' said Laura, wrinkling her nose, 'and she's certain to be busy, she won't thank us for calling, will she? I wonder how much she's upset about Miss Faintley's death?'

They made the cross-country journey by car, with Laura driving. The school, which was well away from the centre of the town, looked pleasantly clean and modern and was surrounded by gardens and its own playing-fields.

Butters, the caretaker, whom Darling had already interviewed, was superintending the unloading of coke for the school furnaces when Mrs Bradley and Laura arrived.

'Did you want someone?' he asked warily, for it was not unknown for the myrmidons of the Education Office to descend upon the school with extraordinary queries and sheaves of official forms just when the head teacher was busiest. 'And don't stick that next load down there, mate,' he added to one of the coalmen. 'That there's a means of egress, if you don't mind me pointing it out, and if you goes and blocks it all up – '

'I would like to speak to Miss Golightly,' said Mrs Bradley. 'Will you kindly direct me to her room if she is in the building? My name is Lestrange Bradley.'

'Very good,' said Butters. He led the way along a short stone corridor and into a cool, dim vestibule. 'That there's her door. You have to knock and then wait for the buzzer.'

Mrs Bradley carried out these instructions and the buzzer's discourteous invitation took her into Miss Golightly's presence. The headmistress was tall, spare and extremely well dressed. She gave an immediate impression of stony-hearted efficiency, her armour, Mrs Bradley supposed, against a world less sensitive than herself.

'Good morning,' she said, looking from Mrs Bradley, small, alert and elderly, to Laura, big, well-built and youthful.

'I have come for some information about the late Miss Faintley, who, I believe, was on the staff here,' Mrs Bradley began.

'Miss Faintley's case is in the hands of the police and they have already been to the school, I understand. May I ask for what purpose you require information about Miss Faintley?'

'Certainly. I am consulting psychiatrist to the Home Office, and there are certain aspects of Miss Faintley's case which I find interesting and which the police are willing that I should investigate.'

'Yes, I see. Won't you sit down? Excuse me just a minute.' She went out of the room and closed the door behind her.

'Gone to her secretary's room to use the other phone and dig up our reputations,' prophesied Laura. 'Sensible woman, that. Tactful, too. Don't want to hurt our feelings.'

'No. And now you'd better leave me alone with her, I think.'

'Right,' agreed Laura cordially. 'I'll go and stroll round the games field. It comes to me with a blast like the crack of doom that I shall find myself on the staff here very shortly!' She cocked an inquiring eye at Mrs Bradley. 'Is that what you were thinking as we came home?'

'I don't know yet,' her employer answered. 'It depends upon what I learn about Miss Faintley to-day.' She waved Laura out into the sunshine and took stock of the room while she awaited Miss Golightly's return.

This was somewhat delayed. When the head teacher reappeared she apologized briefly for leaving her visitor alone so long.

'It wasn't that I doubted you at all, of course, but I get such a number of what I can only feel are casual callers, that I don't really want to waste time on those who don't matter.' She smiled to take the sting out of this home-truth, but Mrs Bradley expressed entire agreement, and plunged straightway into business.

'This, of course, is a co-educational school,' she said. 'May I ask whether the late Miss Faintley had any particular friends among the men on your staff?'

'So far as I am aware she had not. In fact, as soon as I received the news of this dreadful business I sent to Mr Rankin, my first assistant, to ask him the very same question. His reply is here. It came by the next morning's post.'

'What made you send to him, I wonder?'

'I wanted to be prepared for eventualities. I was naturally deeply shocked to learn what had happened, and I realized that the school was bound to be involved. I have noticed that when a woman is found murdered for no apparent reason, the police ask first whether she had any men friends. I have also noticed,' she added tartly, 'that the dead woman never seems to have heard of such creatures as men!'

'Indeed, yes,' agreed Mrs Bradley. 'And Mr Rankin's letter?'

'Ah, yes. Here it is.' Miss Golightly produced a letter post-marked Torquay. Mrs Bradley thanked her and opened the envelope.

'I am most upset,' Mr Rankin had written in a plain, unscholarly hand, 'but can offer no suggestions. Our unfortunate colleague had no entanglements, so far as I am aware, but you will appreciate that her private life was a little outside my scope. As her death occurred on holiday there is every chance that the excitement will soon die down. It would be very bad for the school if it did not. But I really think we need not worry too much, particularly as it all took place such a distance away from Kindleford.'

'It did not take place at such a very great distance away from Mr Rankin's holiday address,' said Mrs Bradley. Miss Golightly looked at her very sharply.

'I hope you are not thinking along *those* sort of lines,' she said firmly. 'I assure you that Mr Rankin is the best of husbands and fathers, and is the last man on earth to entangle himself on holiday, or at any other time, with the women teachers!'

Mrs Bradley nodded. 'I was merely remarking on a coincidence,' she said. 'What can you tell me about a boy of thirteen named Street? He attends this school, I believe.'

'Street? Mark Angus Street? Why, certainly he does. His father is an accountant, and quite comfortably off as our parents go. Mark is an intelligent but somewhat indolent boy. We are hoping he will wake up later and do well. He is between thirteen and fourteen and in the A stream of his year. What did you wish to know about him?'

'He stayed at Miss Faintley's hotel in Cromlech. He was taken by her (at her suggestion) to visit the cathedral city of Torbury, but he lost trace of her there and was present when her body was discovered by my secretary at the top of Cromlech Down.'

'Really? I had no idea of this!'

'No, the boy's name was kept out of the papers. He was not the person who actually discovered the body, and it seemed much better not to involve him.'

'That was extremely thoughtful. Have you seen the boy?'

'Yes, indeed. My secretary and I were staying at the same hotel as the Streets and Miss Faintley herself, although I never saw Miss Faintley alive.'

'Oh, I *see*! No wonder you are interested in the case.'

'Yes.'

'That *would* seem to make a difference, Mrs Bradley, of course. I wonder how best I can help you?'

'By allowing me to ask you one more question. I don't think for a moment that you will be able to answer it, and it is highly confidential, if you don't mind.'

'I am accustomed to regarding myself as a repository of secrets,' said the headmistress with a smile.

'I expect you are. Well, then, do you happen to know whether Miss Faintley was in the habit of collecting parcels from Hagford railway station?'

'In the habit? That is a little too sweeping. She always collected the school stock from there.'

'But you have a station here, haven't you?'

'Yes, but Hagford is a big junction and we are only on a small branch line, and, after some very important material went hopelessly astray once, it was decided that we would leave it at Hagford luggage office and collect it at our convenience. It helps at holiday times, too, if we know it's safely stored and just waiting to be picked up.'

'And Miss Faintley was the collector?'

'Yes. It should be the caretaker's job really, but he has nothing but his bicycle, which isn't any good for the size and number of the packages we get – stationery for the whole school, text-books, art, craft and needlework materials, new hockey sticks by the dozen, and so on – so Miss Faintley, who had her own car, used to act as school carrier. I think the fact that she used to make the journeys in school time made attractive what might otherwise have been a tiresome business. Sometimes she would make the trip three or four times in a single morning, and so, of course, be freed from her classes.'

'That is extremely interesting.'

'I suppose I mayn't ask what makes it interesting?'

'Why not? You have agreed to be discreet, and, besides, as we are to collaborate, I will be as frank with you as the police case will permit.' She gave Miss Golightly a concise account of the story told to the police by young Mr Mandsell. 'And now you see why I asked you whether Miss Faintley had any particular men friends on your staff,' she said in conclusion.

'As to that, neither Mr Rankin nor I seem able to help you. But when school reassembles you had better come along and talk to some of the women on the staff. They will know. And that reminds me of the gap that hasn't been filled yet – and won't be until the next meeting of the Staffing Committee.'

'Miss Faintley's post, of course. What did she teach?'

'Nature study to the younger classes and she helped with the girls' games.'

'Could you arrange for my secretary to take the post

for a couple of weeks? Miss Menzies was trained as a teacher.'

'I should be very glad to have her. It would tide us over nicely. I'll ring the office at once and let them know. They've already told me they can't promise me a Supply, so, if Miss Menzies could cope, that would – '

'Kill two birds with one stone.'

'Yes, yes, of course.' But the headmistress did not look happy. 'I deprecate the choice of metaphor.'

'I wonder,' remarked Mrs Bradley conversationally, 'what school gathering was being held here at the end of the term?'

'Gathering? Oh, the Leaving Dance, you mean! We hold it at the end of the summer term and invite old scholars, the staff past and present, and the two top forms. It is quite informal.'

'Yes. Do all the staff turn up?'

'I have no idea. I'm always extremely busy at the end of the term and although I pop in now and again because the old scholars sometimes like a word and because the children are disappointed if one does not sample the cakes and lemonade, I never inquire who is there or who is not. There is no obligation to attend, as it is not an official school function.'

'Would Mr Rankin know who was there?'

'This year Mr Rankin and Mrs Moles were in here with me checking the stock lists and the needlework accounts. They did go into the hall two or three times, but I doubt whether either of them would know whether the whole staff was there. People drift in and out, you know, come late, go early – that sort of thing. It would be difficult to keep a check, particularly as the hall was crowded. The dance is popular with Old Scholars, and then there were fifty boys and girls there as well.'

'In your opinion, could Mr Rankin have left the building long enough to get to the Park Road telephone-box and back?'

'Definitely not. It takes twenty-five minutes of brisk

walking to get to Park Road from here, and the telephone is half-way down – say another six or seven minutes' walk – and he possesses neither car nor bicycle.'

'Thank you. That is most helpful. Was the staff-room in use during the evening?'

'Oh, yes, of course. There is the cloakroom question, for one thing. And, then, I usually have some special sandwiches and some coffee prepared for the staff. Many of them do not care about cakes and lemonade, and, in any case, need a respite from the revels!'

'And there is a telephone in the staff-room?'

'Yes, there is. The Education Committee were not at all co-operative over that, but I insisted. I was not going to have my teachers feel that I did not trust them to put in their threepences without being watched by me! You would be astonished, Mrs Bradley, at the indignities which certain members of local councils will put on their teachers unless the interests of those teachers are closely watched. "A telephone in the staff-room," I said, "or this is the very last time I make use of mine, and then you will have to write me letters about every little thing." Hard luck on the office, of course. It was not their decision. However, I obtained their co-operation and the staff obtained their telephone, so that was that.'

'Admirable!' said Mrs Bradley. 'Would you be surprised to learn that Miss Faintley may have made the journeys to bring back the school stock a cover for less reputable activities?'

Miss Golightly looked troubled but not surprised.

'I had never thought of such a thing, naturally,' she replied. 'I trust my staff implicitly. One must. But the news of her death has been so disturbing, and the reason for it so mysterious that I am prepared to believe almost anything of her now. You mean that she was not necessarily an innocent victim? There were . . . *reasons* for her death?'

'It begins to look like it. She is known to have taken parcels from Hagford to a small shop kept by a man named

Tomson, who does not appear altogether to be *persona grata* with the police.'

'Oh, dear! This is worse than I thought. It will be very bad for the school if all this comes out, as I suppose it is bound to do.'

'I don't know. Miss Faintley may have been a cat's-paw. That is the theory at present.'

'Then it doesn't say much for her brains and character. Well, as I cannot be of further assistance . . .'

She smiled, to terminate the interview, and opened the door. Mrs Bradley collected Laura and informed her of the fate in store.

CHAPTER EIGHT

KINDLEFORD SCHOOL

*

'And the treason, too long pent,
To his ears was evident.
The young deities discuss'd
Laws of form and metre just,
Orb, quintessence, and sunbeams,
What subsisteth and what seems.'

RALPH WALDO EMERSON – *Uriel*

THE first person Laura noticed as she entered the school playground was Mark. She had not bargained for this. She would have to teach Mark; she might have to rebuke or even punish him; she would have to forget their previous alliance and the easy and confidential fabric of which it had been built, and, above all, she would have to forget (and, what was much more difficult, see to it that Mark forgot, too) that she and he had been together when she found Miss Faintley's body.

Slightly to her resentment, it appeared that Miss Golightly had foreseen these complications and was prepared to deal with them in what Laura deemed to be her characteristic fashion.

Laura had acknowledged Mark's salute and shy grin with a nod, and had gone straight to the head teacher's room to report that she had arrived and was prepared to begin her duties. Miss Golightly greeted her charmingly, produced the school time-table, explained Laura's part in it shortly and comprehensibly, showed her a list of school duties which included keeping a milk and dinner list, officiating in the playground during break, taking her turn at dinner duty, supervision of the cloakrooms, the banning of chewing-gum and strip-cartoon papers (for all), facial adornment (for the girls), lethal weapons (for the boys), fountain-pens (for both sexes), and likewise personal bottles of ink. There was also the more debatable matter of gymnastics on the cloak-room bars and pegs, and the shoo-ing off of all children from the school premises when school was over except for such as claimed to be (*a*) going to the lavatory because they were being put in detention; (*b*) required for choir practice, dramatic club, games practice or any other recognized out-of-school activity; or (*c*) waiting (a nuisance this, but un-avoidable, it appeared) for the bus to take them to the outlying villages from which they were separated each school day.

'Fun and games, in fact,' commented Laura cheerfully. 'All right, Miss Golightly. Fair enough. What a ghastly life kids lead, when one comes to think of it! Harried, chivvied, overruled and put upon! I'm glad I'm as old as I am. How do *you* feel about it?'

Miss Golightly smiled sourly, but Laura, accustomed to Mrs Bradley's leering, intimidating grins, was not im-pressed. Miss Golightly sensed this, and her smile altered and became amiable.

'I entirely agree with you, Miss Menzies,' she replied.

'Grand! Now, touching a matter of some slight em-barrassment to himself and me – '

'I shall see Street,' said the headmistress. 'You need anticipate no difficulty there. You get his form once a week only. Out of school there will naturally be no contact.'

'Unless the police case calls for it,' said Laura. 'That seems to sum things up,' she added brightly. 'And now, what about the botany syllabus?'

Miss Golightly opened a drawer and handed over a type-script. Laura glanced at it.

'Can do,' she said. 'How do you like it taught? – "How doth the little busy bee?" – or a list of natural orders, with appropriate information attached, all done out nice and proper in our little notebooks?'

'You'll soon see!' snapped Miss Golightly, and, with this intensely human reaction, she gained a place in Laura's affections which she was destined not to lose. 'And it's ten minutes to nine,' she added. 'Time you were in your little classroom! At break I will introduce you to the rest of the staff.'

She conducted Laura to a room on the ground floor of the school, introduced her briefly to a mixed class of twelve-year-old children and left her. Laura was equal to the situation.

'All right,' she said. 'Who's the form captain?'

Two children, a boy and a girl, stood up amid comments from the rest of the class.

'Right,' said Laura. 'After break I shall want to know who are the window monitors, the milk monitors, the dinner monitors, the door monitor, the cupboard monitors, the general scavengers, the fort-holder, the flower monitor, the blackboard monitor, the hymn-book monitor, the teacher's yes-man, the teacher's pest, the liaison monitor, and the person who wrote the words on the outside window-ledge of this classroom.'

A girl put up her hand. Laura looked at her sourly.

'Please, miss,' said the girl, 'what's a fort-holder?'

'Ah, that,' said Laura. 'I'm glad you asked me that. I gather that you are teacher's yes-man, so that's one problem solved. A fort-holder, as you ought to know, and probably do know, at your age, is the stooge who stands at the classroom door when teacher has gone out of the room, remains on guard during the consequent chaos, and sings out at the appropriate moment, "Shut up, you twerps! She's coming!" And upon the strength of my personality,' Laura concluded, 'depends whether the twerps shut up or whether they don't . . . a point which will soon be established. And now you can all get down to the hall for morning assembly, and heaven help the one who is out of line by the time that *I* get down there.'

The allocation of text-books, stationery, pens, ink, blotting-paper, rulers, compasses, protractors, set-squares, and copies of the form time-table occupied the time pleasantly and noisily until break. Laura saw the class out and went in search of the staff-room. She was almost run into at one end of the corridor by a stout, florid, middle-aged man in a suit of shiny-seated navy-blue, who said:

'Hah! The new recruit, eh? My name's Tomalin. English master and so forth. Let me guide you towards the coffee and biscuits.'

'My name is Menzies,' Laura responded. 'Thank you very much. But I thought,' she added, as they walked along the corridor towards the staircase which led to the staff-room, 'that somebody called Cardillon took English.'

'Oh, well, actually, yes, of course, she does. That's to say, we run a G.C.E. course here and so have to take on these young lady B.A.s. Unfortunately, in my opinion. They may have been to a university, and all that, but when it comes to a spot of honest spade-work, there's nobody like the good old choked-in-the-chalk-dust practitioner to ram it home good and solid. Up here, and look out for boys rushing round corners and jumping down eight stairs at a time. They're not supposed to, but they *will* do it. Miss Golightly's too soft. Now, if *I* were a headmaster . . . as I should have been, years before this, if kissing didn't go by favour, which, in this blasted job, it does, and always will do . . . well, here we are.'

He gave the partly-open door a push with his foot, and Laura found herself in a biggish, square room with a fire-place, a gas-oven, a large table and three small ones, a Dutch wardrobe, two bookcases, several armchairs and even more small chairs, a chaise-longue, a large waste-paper basket, a nest of lockers, and a photograph of the Roman Colosseum. Enamel trays covered most of the surface of the large table and, when Laura entered, the coffee was being poured out by two schoolgirls whilst a third carried round the filled cups.

Mr Tomalin made no attempt to introduce Laura. He charged up to the table, collected a cup of coffee from the girl who was about to pass it to one of the mistresses, grabbed two biscuits from an open tin which stood beside one of the trays, planted one of them in his mouth and the other on his saucer, fished in his waistcoat pocket for a couple of saccharine tablets, dropped them in his cup and made for a vacant chair.

A grey-haired, quiet-voiced man came forward from where he had been standing with his back against a radiator.

'Good morning,' he said. 'May I introduce myself? I'm Rankin, senior assistant. Miss Golightly has a parent, so she asked me to do the honours.'

The bedlam into which Laura had been ushered by Mr Tomalin had calmed down. Raised voices were lowered. Mr Rankin slightly raised his.

'Miss Menzies,' he said. 'Mrs Moles, Miss Cardillon, Miss Franks, Miss Batt, Miss Ellersby, Miss Welling, Mr Taylor, Mr Roberts, Mr Tomalin, Mr Fennison, Mr Trench. I won't bother with what we all teach. You'll find out soon enough. Perhaps,' he continued, in a lowered tone as the babble broke out afresh, 'Miss Cardillon, you'd give Miss Menzies the low-down. Cissie, some coffee for Miss Menzies. That's the style. Help yourself to the biscuits, Miss Menzies. If you take sugar I'm afraid you'll have to provide it for yourself. We get a tea and a milk allowance, but that's all.' He raised his voice again. 'By the way, we seem to be all here. Who's on playground duty?'

Miss Welling and Mr Taylor, who had hoped, on the first day of term, to escape this loathsome task, betook themselves to the open spaces, there, presumably, to make more difficult the art of mayhem and to cause litter to be cleared up, washbasins emptied and chains pulled. In the staff-room the flood tide of post-holiday conversation welled up once more. Miss Cardillon led Laura to a chair. She was a tall, fair-skinned, freckled woman in her thirty-second year, and Laura liked the look and sound of her as much as she had disliked the look and sound of the mediocre, disgruntled Mr Tomalin.

'It's a bigger staff than I should have thought,' she said, in order to open the conversation.

'Yes. Miss Golightly cuts a good deal of ice at the office, thank goodness, so we're pretty well looked after. It makes a good deal of difference to the non-teaching time we get, and, with a subject like mine – six sets of essays a week, among other things – it's rather useful to have a few periods off to do the marking.'

The break, all too short, came to an end on these words, and Laura asked, as she went down the stairs with Miss Cardillon, 'What about lunch, by the way? Are we all on duty?'

'Oh, no, there's a rota and you won't be put on it yet. We always give the new ones a chance to get acclimatized before the extraneous duties begin. But you can have canteen lunch if you want it.'

'I don't, really,' Laura confessed.

'Good. Let's do the local pub, then. It's the only place in Kindleford where one can get a decent meal, and Miss Golightly doesn't mind. She goes home to lunch herself, most days, and leaves Rankin in charge. He's a married man with kids, so he's quite glad to get a free meal. If you're on duty you don't pay, you see. Well, here we part until twelve. Don't forget to see your girls and Tomalin's girls round the cloakroom. He looks after both sets of boys. And chivvy the little brutes, otherwise they'll be all day, and the dinner hour is short enough as it is.'

Laura went into her classroom to discover that the zealous ink-monitor had overfilled most of the inkwells, a feat which was greeted joyously by the boys and with shrill disgust by the girls. Ink pellets began to fly. There were tears over ink-spotted frocks. Laura went into action, clouted heads, cursed the ink-monitor and ruined the blackboard duster. She had restored order, however, just as Mr Tomalin, with the unctuous crocodile sympathy of one colleague for the disciplinary troubles of another, came into the room without knocking. He carried a cane.

'I thought I heard a noise,' he remarked to the un-naturally silent class.

'Yes, you did,' said Laura, loudly and clearly. 'I am sorry

if we disturbed you. I am not an advocate of free discipline, but I am opposed' – she eyed the cane sternly – 'to a show of weakness masquerading as strength.'

'Oh, well, *I'm* a believer in corporal punishment,' said Mr Tomalin, taken aback by her tone as much as by her words. Laura glanced at her tingling palm and then at several unnaturally red left ears in the front row on the boys' side of the class, and suddenly laughed.

'I can't stand that man Tomalin next door to me,' she said to Miss Cardillon when they met to go out to lunch.

'Think yourself lucky you're not me,' retorted Miss Cardillon with unprofessional frankness. '*I* have to share my subject with him, and by the time I get his classes the kids are fed up and sick to their little bellies of composition, grammar, and Eng. lit. I'd throw up my job except that I've had a hot tip that I'm to be short-listed for the next headship. So don't talk about Tomalin to *me*!'

This set Laura's thoughts in the direction of her real duty in the school.

'That reminds me,' she said. 'Do we refer to the others just by surnames? I mean, do the men talk of you as Cardillon, Miss Cardillon, a nickname, or how?'

'They call me Liz, behind my back. So do most of the boys.'

'Liz?'

'Short for Skinny Lizzie,' explained Miss Cardillon cheerfully. 'On the other hand, if I were ringing up the school to explain that I couldn't come, or if I were out on a school visit and had some reason to ring up, I should inevitably say, *Cardillon speaking*. It's considered rather Fauntleroy to call yourself *Miss* Cardillon on a mixed staff.' Miss Ellersby and Miss Franks, who were joining them to make up a table for four, concurred in this opinion.

'It doesn't do to call too much attention to the blessed state of spinsterhood in *this* school,' Miss Ellersby, an anaemic, sardonic-eyed woman of forty, added. 'Although we only get four-fifths of the men's money and work three times as hard as most of them, we're looked upon as bloated plutocrats. What I say is, you can't have a wife and still expect to have holidays in sunny Italy. Selfish brutes! They ought to try *our* lives for a bit! Digs and landladies, or else a flat and your own shopping and chores! If it weren't for the holidays, I should go crackers, for one!'

'I don't know,' said Miss Golightly, coming into Laura's first 'nature' lesson, 'whether you would care to call for the next parcel of school stock? It is just as you like, of course. Elbows, Frances! Handkerchief, Evans!'

The two children looked so much astonished at being thus addressed that Laura guessed that these injunctions were not Miss Golightly's usual line of country. The head, she thought, was embarrassed, an uncommon state of affairs and one which indicated clearly that, a conscientious and intelligent woman, she fully realized that to offer Laura the task which possibly had brought Miss Faintley to her death was to take advantage of the possession of authority, a thing she never knowingly did. She added, very quickly:

'I can easily make other arrangements, but, as I know quite well why you are here, I thought perhaps it would offer facilities if – '

'I'd like it very much,' said Laura warmly. 'When would you wish me to go?'

'It could be to-morrow morning, I think. I have been looking at the time-table. You have only one nature lesson. It is with 1B. They can draw instead, and Mr Tomalin, who is free then, can sit with them while he marks his books. You have your own form for the rest of the time. They can have an extra arithmetic lesson and then do silent reading. You might set them a chapter which they can prepare for an essay. That is only a suggestion, of course, but it is as well to set before them some definite objective, otherwise they only waste their time. How are things going? Quite well?'

'More or less, thank you. Getting hold of all their names is the worst part.'

'Get the children to make out nameplates which they can

leave out on the desk until you get to know them. Very well, then. To-morrow, as soon as you have called the register and sent the class down to morning assembly, knock on my door and I will give you the invoices. But you *will* be careful, won't you? I should be dreadfully sorry if you did anything rash, as it appears poor Miss Faintley must have done.'

The moment she was gone there was a buzz all over the classroom, for, although both teachers had talked very quietly, the elastic-eared young had followed most of the conversation.

'Now what?' asked Laura, who had been giving a good lesson until the entrance of the headmistress. The buzz ceased, but one or two hissing whispers went the rounds, and then a voice from the back row said threateningly:

'Go on, Maisie Dukes! I dare you! You said you would. Now you go on and do it!'

'What *is* all this?' asked Laura, mentally prepared to deal with impudence. A girl in the second row got up, flushed and inclined to giggle. Laura deduced that she was scared.

'Please, Miss Menzies,' she said half-hysterically, 'some of them think you're a policewoman!'

'Well, you can assure them that I am not!' said Laura, grinning. 'But don't bank too steeply on that!'

'Did you read about Miss Faintley in the papers?' asked a bright-eyed girl from a front desk. 'We thought anybody what took her place must be a policewoman trying to find out things. That's what *Too Pretty for Prison* was about.'

'Was it? Why don't you read something decent?'

Howls of protest from the girls and of derision (equally divided between Laura and the girls) from the boys greeted this question. Laura became terse and authoritative, and the lesson continued. But she had broken the thread of it, and her mind was occupied with other matters. She wondered how much the children knew about Miss Faintley. Probably a good deal more than the staff did, since they would have regarded her more dispassionately, less sympathetically (most likely) and were keener observers and more accomplished critics. A pity that she could not talk to them freely. There might be something extremely important to be gained. They might even know which member of the staff was the most likely to have been Miss Faintley's friend of the telephone-box arrangements. A pity one couldn't very well ask them!

Another aspect occurred to her. She remembered, from her own schooldays, the capacity of adolescents for imaginative speculation. If these children were inclined to the belief that she was connected with the police it was only a matter of time before they found out that their guess was not so very far from the truth, and once that was established her value to Mrs Bradley as a spy in the school camp would be questionable if not actually non-existent.

Somewhere in the class a languid hand wagged feebly. Startled, Laura came to herself, to discover that while her conscious mind had been occupied with other, and, she felt, graver matters, her subconscious mind had been presenting the class with a résumé of social life in the early eighteenth century, the botany lesson, rather oddly, having hitched itself on to this subject.

'Well?' she said, scowling at the hand. Its owner dropped it, rose to her feet and inquired:

'Did you say *copy* or *coffee*?'

'I said *idiot*,' replied Laura. 'Sit down and attend properly.' She looked at the clock. 'Five minutes to put down in your jotting-books a summary of the lesson. Shortest effort has to be read aloud by whoever passes it in.'

The shortest effort ran as follows:

'The pea and bean are dicotyledons and are often eaten. Queen Anne's favourite drink was coffee. She built many houses to contain it and these were taken over by George I. He blew a South Sea Bubble and Lloyd's was floated. It afterwards became a bank. The bank clerks were called underwriters. The top writers sank ships and the underwriters had to pay. They said how much they could afford, and a Lenten bell was rung.'

The author of this essay was asked to remain behind, as she had refused to read it aloud. She confided to Laura that she was shy. She added that she was sorry, but she had to fetch her little brother from the infants' school. He was not allowed to cross the High Street alone. She spoke reasonably, without impertinence, and finished tearfully, 'I couldn't read it out to them boys!'

'Quite right, too,' agreed Laura. 'All right then. Cut along. After all, why should *you* suffer because I give a rotten lesson?'

'Hullo, hullo!' said Mr Tomalin, appearing in Laura's doorway as the girl hurried out after the others. 'Been having trouble with Susan Hopkins? She's an impudent little baggage. You don't want to put up with any nonsense.'

'I don't intend to,' replied Laura, who considered that it was high time to settle Mr Tomalin's hash. 'And if you don't mind my saying so, will you kindly leave me to manage my own affairs? I am far more capable of dealing with adolescent girls than you are!'

'Here, here, I *say!*' protested Mr Tomalin, indicating the cupboard monitors.

'Go and say it somewhere else,' retorted Laura. She turned and began to put her books into her desk. She had behaved with impropriety, she knew; if she had not known, stifled giggles and whispers from the cupboard would have told her. 'I shall never make a teacher,' she told Mrs Bradley that evening in the Stone House, to which she had driven as soon as school was over. Mrs Bradley, however, was well satisfied. Laura had established one important point and had made a valuable contact. It seemed almost certain that Miss Faintley's correspondent on the telephone had been a member of the school staff, and Laura was already in a position to test for herself, in circumstances which could scarcely arouse suspicion, the relationship, if there was one, between the school parcels and those of less orthodox character which Miss Faintley had collected from Hagford Junction.

Mrs Bradley did not agree with Laura that anything would have been gained if the schoolchildren could be questioned about Miss Faintley.

'All you would acquire,' she said, with her crocodile grin, 'would be a scurrilous suggestion from the boys that Miss Faintley was a victim of "maiden virtue rudely strumpeted" and from the girls the equally romantic theory that her boy-friend killed her in a fit of jealousy. All these children read such Sunday papers as specialize in these matters.'

'Yes, I suppose they do. Incidentally, I'm by way of making an enemy on the staff. That man Tomalin. I bit his head off to-day for not minding his own business. He's had the impudence to try to keep order for me and to impress upon me not to stand cheek from the kids.'

'Misdirected chivalry, don't you think?'

'No, I don't! I know it isn't. It's just sheer showing off and nosey-parkering. He's a washout himself and his only way of trying to prove that he isn't is this attitude of pretending that other people are even more inefficient than he is! He gets under my skin!'

'A waste of nervous energy on your part, dear child. Besides, a sense of inferiority and a disappointing professional life are not calculated to bring out the best in any man.'

'That's all very well!' retorted Laura, looking in the mirror at her own flushed face and beginning to laugh. 'You don't have to put up with him! I *do!*'

'What are the rest of the staff like?'

'Pretty mixed. I don't know an awful lot about them yet, and I'm as far off as ever from finding out which of the men was in with Miss Faintley over that business of the parcels.'

'It's early days yet to begin worrying about that. Later on, the police may be able to prise the information out of that (I am certain) villainous shopkeeper. And how go the biology lessons?'

'Nature study – so-called. We don't go in for biology. I think Miss Golightly feels it's out of place in a mixed school, and I'm not at all sure she isn't right. Sex-education, which is all that biology seems to add up to in modern schools, is the expense of embarrassment in a waste of muddled idealism, to my way of thinking. With which unpardonable bowdlerizing of the Bard I will break off in order to ask what's for dinner to-night, a subject of considerably greater importance to me at the moment than any academic discussion of What Shall We Teach and How Shall We Teach it. Don't you think so yourself? – or aren't you hungry?'

CHAPTER NINE

MR BANNISTER

*

'A Venus' imp thou hast brought forth, so steadfast and
so sage.'

NICHOLAS GRIMALD – *A True Love*

LAURA had had, during the night watches (for she was a
person who required but an hour or two of sleep) what she
thought was a very good idea. She drove into Kindleford,
carried out Miss Golightly's instructions, and then, armed
with the invoices, drove to Miss Faintley's aunt and asked
permission to use Miss Faintley's car. She explained that it
would cause less comment at the Junction than if she went
in her own.

The aunt was in bed, however, and had been in bed ever
since the last visit of the police. She was prostrate with grief
and worry, declared the daily woman. As to Miss Faintley's
car, that was in the garage in Long Hill Street, and the
police had the key, and the woman could not go and worry
Miss Faintley about it, nor with nothing else, for the matter
of that. Prostrate she was, poor thing, and who could
wonder at it?

Laura drove to the police station (she was, in any case,
under Mrs Bradley's instructions to acquaint Inspector
Darling with the fact that she was going to Hagford to
collect stock for the school), introduced herself and gave
Mrs Bradley's message and the information that she had
tried to borrow Miss Faintley's car and had failed. None of
this appeared to interest Darling. He doodled idly on his
blotting-paper while she talked and then said abruptly:

'Very good, miss. We'll make a note of it. You'll be

going straight back to the school with the parcel, I don't doubt.'

'I don't see anything else to do.'

'No, miss. Well,' he looked up and smiled, 'don't go running into trouble. I hear you're a teacher at the school now, taking Miss Faintley's place. We had Mrs Bradley on the telephone last night. It appears pretty certain that Miss Faintley was expecting to speak to another member of the staff that night she spoke to Mr Mandsell. We could do with knowing who that teacher was, miss.'

'I know. I'll do my best to find out.'

'It may not help us, of course. May just have been somebody who was willing to do Miss Faintley a favour. Still, it would clear up one small point for us, and every little helps. According to what Mrs Bradley found out from Miss Golightly, it couldn't have been Mr Rankin. Not that I'd ever think it could be. I know Bob Rankin well. The last man on earth to get mixed up in any funny business. Bannister, too, is a very reliable chap.'

Laura's brief acquaintance with Mr Rankin was sufficient to cause her to agree heartily with this point of view. In another two minutes she was in her own car and making for Hagford Junction. The journey took less than ten minutes, for the road was clear and fairly straight, and Laura pulled up outside the station entrance with no idea of how she was going to approach her real objective . . . the gaining of information about Miss Faintley and the parcels which had not been intended for the school.

The left luggage office was in charge of a round-faced, ingenuous-looking porter who was afflicted with stammering speech.

'K-K-Kindleford Sc-Sc-School? I'll s-s-see.'

'Are you always in charge here?' asked Laura, as she signed for three large packages.

'Y-y-yes, of c-c-course I am.'

'Liar!' thought Laura, who had been told about the missing brothers Price.

'Remember Miss Faintley who used to come here?'

The porter's blue eyes bulged.

'M-m-murdered on h-h-holiday?'

'Yes. What about those other parcels she used to collect? You know, the ones that were addressed to her personally, and not to the school.'

'Oh, them! Well, there's one h-here, but it's marked *To Be Left Till Called For*.'

'Well, I'm calling for it,' Laura said blithely. The detective fever she had experienced during her abortive inquiries in Torbury were fired afresh. She saw herself driving triumphantly back to the Stone House at Wandles Parva bearing a parcel which, when unwrapped by Mrs Bradley, would disclose the whole secret of Miss Faintley's untimely death, the full villainy of Tomson, the identity of the men who had removed the case of ferns, and the entire foolishness of the novelist Geoffrey Mandsell.

But the porter, stammering and nervous, refused to consider the idea that Laura should make herself responsible for the parcel, and, as she was not in a position to compel him to part with it, she had to drive back to school with nothing but the three heavy packages of stock.

On the way she rang up Mrs Bradley and reported upon her failure to secure the private parcel.

'I'm very glad you *haven't* got it,' said Mrs Bradley calmly. 'Tell the police it is there. I don't want you knocked on the head. Did you actually see it?'

'Well, I think I know which it was. It was flat and rectangular, like a photograph or something.'

With considerable *chagrin* Laura rang up the police station, but it appeared that the stammering porter had been before her. He had reported that a woman teacher had called for the school parcels and that she had tried to get hold of one to which she was not entitled. A police car had already gone to Hagford. Laura was thanked for her telephone message. She returned to school, thoroughly disgruntled.

'Takes you some time to get to Hagford and back! Car have a breakdown?' Miss Cardillon inquired at break.

'No. Dumped the stock and went off on a toot.'

'Miss Golightly was rather upset. Sent a couple of kids to search the place for you. Faintley used to get back in under the hour. What *have* you been a-doing of? Did you get lost, or something?'

'I've been to telephone, that's all.'

'Well, silly, there's a telephone in the staff-room. Why on earth not pop up and use that?'

'Somebody would have been in there marking books or a couple of kids getting coffee ready.'

'Oh, yes, there's always that snag. Oh, Lord! It's time already! These breaks don't seem to last any time at all. Coming out to lunch again to-day?'

'Yes, of course. I say, some time or other, tell me a bit about Miss Faintley. The luggage clerk at the station . . . well, at the left luggage office . . . mentioned her when I picked up the stock.'

'Faintley? You'd better ask Batt. She knew her better than anyone, except perhaps Franks. What did the porter say? . . . Naturally, we've all discussed the murder *ad nauseam*, and the thing is a complete mystery. According to the papers, robbery wasn't the motive, but nobody can think of another. But come on. The lines will be leading in. I wish we could troop into school in a civilized sort of way, but Rankin won't have it. Says the boys would create hell. In spite of a soft voice and respectable manners, he's very much one of the old brigade and a bit of a martinet.'

'"The great thing for boys is discipline, sonny, discipline,"' quoted Laura under her breath. Miss Cardillon laughed and they went their ways. Four classes had games lessons that afternoon, so Laura was in a fine strategic position to inveigle Miss Batt into talking about Miss Faintley.

'Yes, I shall miss her,' said Miss Batt. 'I do all the P.T. for the girls, but she used to help with the games. I'm jolly glad you're able to step into the breach.'

'What was she like?' asked Laura. They were changing into shirts and shorts in the staff cloakroom, for Miss

Golightly had arranged that the physical training staff should have a free half hour before they went on to the games field, where they were to spend the rest of the afternoon.

'Like? Oh, I don't know. Quiet and not exactly exciting. A good enough teacher, I suppose. Didn't get on very well with the boys. She wasn't much good at coaching hockey or tennis, either, but she volunteered to help in the games lessons because then she had only the girls. I don't really know an awful lot about her, apart from that. I mean, we didn't meet out of school.'

'Did she quarrel with people much?'

'You're thinking about the murder. I keep on thinking about it, too. We all do, as I say. It's a real mystery. I mean, one knows about these cosh gangs and awful people, but it doesn't seem to have been that sort of thing at all. Not that the papers tell you much. If you ask me, the police haven't a clue, but, of course, they won't tell that to the reporters. As to quarrelling – no. She kept herself to herself, as they say.'

'I suppose' – Laura hesitated, but there seemed no necessity for finesse – 'I suppose she wasn't mixed up with a man?'

'A man?' Miss Batt looked up with a hockey boot still in her hand. 'Good heavens, no!'

'Not even somebody on the staff here?'

'Well, you've met them all. Rankin, Trench and Tomalin are stodgily, respectably married, Taylor and Roberts share a flat and a housekeeper and care about nothing but making film-strips, Bannister is a complete woman-hater and lives for the holidays, when he goes off on his own and climbs down into potholes, and Fennison, my opposite number, is crazy about a girl called Penny Stretton who's been steadily refusing him (or so he tells us) for the past three years, so he's taken to table tennis and intends to win an open championship. Besides, if you'd only *known* Faintley . . .! She wasn't any Cleopatra, I can tell you!'

She resumed her occupation of putting on her hockey boots.

'Yes,' said Laura, 'it doesn't sound like a *crime passionel*. Well, what are the alternatives?'

'You tell me, while I recline on the sofa thing in the staff-room and put on a fag. We've all talked our hindlegs off about it. It just seems to be one of those things. A maniac, as likely as not. I don't see any other explanation.'

'Did she usually go on holiday alone?'

'*Was* she alone, then? Nothing was said about that. I thought she barged about with an aunt? I know she lived with one, because she was always grousing about the aunt being extravagant with coal and electric light. Have one of these horrible fags. We've got plenty of time. I always give the kids ten minutes to get changed and serve themselves out with the hockey sticks and coloured bands. They make hell, but Miss Golightly can't hear 'em!'

Laura enjoyed the rest of the afternoon. She was a good games player herself and a first-class coach. As soon as time was called, she went off to change, and, by good luck, ran into Miss Franks. Miss Franks was the art mistress. Her main emotional outlet was her bitter, unceasing warfare with Mrs Moles, the needlework teacher, for each thought that the other's subject should be the inferior one. Miss Franks objected strongly to being commanded to improvise embroidery patterns on squared paper for the benefit of Mrs Moles' decorative stitchery classes, and Mrs Moles considered all pure art, as opposed to applied art (i.e., embroidery and stencilling), to be a waste of time, materials, and effort.

'I say,' said Laura, 'how did you and Miss Faintley correlate your subjects? As I'm taking her place I wondered whether you could give me a wrinkle or two about black-board drawings and classroom posters and so forth.'

Miss Franks, who was a small, dark, volatile Jewess, shrugged and smiled.

'I didn't help Faintley,' she said. 'She was old-fashioned. I know what you want, though, and if you will let me send back Trumper if I have the feeling I cannot bear him any longer in my lesson, I will do the drawings for you myself.'

'It's a bargain. Thanks a lot. As for Trumper, I propose to deal with that youth in a manner which will stay with him for the rest of his days. He's a prize toad, and no fate is too black for him. Send him back every time, and I'll guarantee to make his life hell.'

'Thank you very much. Would you like some drawings put up ready for to-morrow?'

During the ensuing forty minutes it turned out that although Miss Franks had never openly quarrelled with Miss Faintley, the budding friendship between them had withered and died.

'Of course I am not Communist,' said Miss Franks, 'but who can expect I should be Nazi? Besides, she was wanting me to lend her money. Well, I am quite willing to be obliging, but to lend money to somebody older than your-self and higher up the scale of salaries, does it make sense?'

'How much?' asked Laura bluntly. Miss Franks looked at her appraisingly and decided to trust her.

'Four hundred pounds,' she said softly. 'Four hundred beautiful pounds. I had not got it, and, even if I had –'

'Oh, Lord! I *quite* agree,' said Laura. 'But why on earth did she want it?'

'Some garbled story of the mortgage, but I found out she was not *buying* anything, only renting, do you see? So I said to myself that here comes something funny. So I don't visit there any more. Anyway, only margarine on the bread, and nothing better than bloaters or a pot of shrimp paste for our tea. There, now.' She stepped away from her work. 'How does that do, would you say?'

'Fine! Thanks a lot. I say, I couldn't do anything like that in a hundred years! How would it be if I made some reason of my own not to send Master Trumper to you at all?'

'That would not pass with Miss Golightly, but it is the kind thought that counts. He slings poster paint about and puts it on other children. He painted Annie Maggs blue last week.'

'I'll paint him *black* and blue,' said Laura, on a note of sadistic enjoyment.

'And that's as far as we got,' reported Laura that evening. 'I don't see what good I'm doing at the school, and it's an intolerably lousy job. Thank goodness it's only for a fortnight! I couldn't stick a whole term.'

'You don't feel you have missed your vocation?'

'No, I jolly well don't! Look here, what *is* the explanation of that man who came out of the telephone-box that night when Mandsell agreed to collect the parcel? And why wouldn't that porter give *me* one? Scared about the murder, I suppose.'

'Ah, the parcel!' said Mrs Bradley. 'Yes. The police collected it, and Inspector Darling was good enough to call me up this afternoon and tell me what was in it.'

'No! Say on! What is it that's so fascinating about parcels?'

'Their mysterious and secret nature. There was a statue in the parcel . . . a piece of plaster representing a slightly inebriated young gentleman in evening cloak and opera hat. When you are at school to-morrow I shall drive in to Kindleford, I think. There are three things I want to do. I want to see the statue and talk to the Inspector; I want to talk to Mr Mandsell, and I think I would like to visit the wicked shopkeeper.'

'Too bad! And there shall I be teaching wretched kids about the lesser hogweed and the greater bladderwort! Our botany syllabus belongs to the age of faith and not of reason. In other words, it's at least forty years out of date. I suspect that Miss Faintley botched it up from what she remembered of her own schooldays. You never knew such silly muck!'

'Never mind. There is something else you can do. Find out, as circumspectly as possible, exactly which of the staff did, and which did not, put in an appearance at that end-of-term party. *Somebody* on the staff knows that Miss Faintley used to deliver those parcels, and I'd rather *we* found out than the police, and so would you.'

'You'd be far better than I at that sort of game. Couldn't we change places for the day?'

'No. I have forgotten all I ever knew about the lesser

hogweed. Besides, the Inspector won't talk to you as he is going to talk to me. But be of good cheer! At the end of next week, unless our problem is solved, we are going back to Cromlech to continue our investigation from there.'

'Lovely! All right, then. I'll continue to wrestle with kids and conscience for another few days. I know now why T.G.I.F. is the harassed teacher's favourite slogan! I wonder . . .'

'Yes?'

'I wonder whether Bannister could help us? He's supposed to be a woman-hater, so he may have a line on Faintley that the others haven't got.'

'You could try, but I think the first step will be to establish which of the staff were and which were not at that end-of-term dance.'

'All right. I can pump Cardillon on that. I'd have done it before, but she's rather intelligent and I want to do it so that she doesn't realize I'm pumping her. Any suggestions?'

'Yes. Take her into your confidence if you discover that she herself was present the whole time at the dance. If she was not, she won't be of very much help. She may, however, be able to tell you of somebody who *was* there the whole time.'

Laura tackled Miss Cardillon on the following morning before school began. She was lucky enough to find her alone in her classroom. It was a golden opportunity.

'I say,' she said, 'when is half-term?'

'I don't know. We haven't had the list round yet.'

'I hope this isn't a school where we're expected to take parties of kids out, or run an Old Scholars' evening, or something of that kind, in the half-term break?'

'Oh, no. We have the Old Scholars twice . . . just before Christmas and at the end of the summer term.'

'Does everybody turn up? I shouldn't know any Old Scholars, you see.'

'It's optional . . . although, of course, Rankin does push it a bit to make sure that enough of us are here to make the thing go.'

'How about you? Do you roll along?'

'Oh, yes. It seems part of the job. We're not asked to do much in the way of outside activities. Miss Golightly's pretty reasonable like that, and I'm one of those who can be led but hates being driven, so I feel it's the thing to show willing.'

'Pity everybody doesn't think the same, but my experience is that the willing horses always do the pulling for the slackers, especially in jobs like this.'

'Yes, that's pretty true. We don't have much bother here, though. Miss Ellersby and Mr Trench are the only ones who never turn up to anything. She's got an ancient father and he's got an invalid wife, so we can't say much, although we feel sometimes that their troubles aren't really our business.'

'Were they the only two who didn't come to the end-of-term dance, then?'

'Oh, well, except for Bannister. He never comes to dances. Says he hates them. Everybody else turned up either for the whole or part of the time, and on the evening in question Mrs Moles stayed on to help in checking the needlework accounts. But what's all this in aid of? There's something behind it. I've an instinct in these matters.'

'Quite so. I'll come clean on two conditions.'

'This sounds interesting.'

'It is. I'm not really a teacher, as you've probably guessed by now, although I was properly trained, but, before I say more, you've got to promise that not one word of this goes a step further . . . Miss Golightly knows it already, so *that* needn't trouble your conscience . . . and, then, you've got to give me the names of at least two people who can swear that you were here the whole evening at that dance.'

'Heavens alive! It sounds like a spy story!'

'That's just what it may be. I'm not, as I say, quite what I seem.'

'Well, of course, I won't breathe a word, and, as for the witnesses, well, Batt, Fennison, and I were running the thing, so we could all swear to one another. Then Welling, as cookery teacher, was in charge of all the refreshments, so she, and her helper, Franks, would have been on the premises all the time, too, if that's any good to you. And now, do relieve my curiosity or I shall burst! It's about Faintley, isn't it? Are you a female sleuth? I don't believe it!'

'I am and I'm not.' Laura gave a full account of how she and Mrs Bradley had first become involved in Miss Faintley's affairs, and she had only just finished when it was time to go to her classroom. She was delighted, however, with the information she had received. It seemed that most people on the staff could be written off so far as the telephone call was concerned. Of the others, it was in the highest degree unlikely that the plump and shrill-voiced Miss Ellersby, the rather unsuitable music specialist, could have impersonated a man, so Laura decided that she also could be passed over. There remained, as possible collaborators with Miss Faintley over the affair of the parcels, Messrs Taylor, Roberts, Bannister, Trench, and Tomalin. Therefore it had been a real man, and not a masquerading woman, who had walked away from the telephone on the night when Mandsell had taken the call intended for somebody else . . . not that Laura had ever thought otherwise. One thing only nagged at her. She felt that if Miss Faintley had expected to hear the voice of a colleague, she must have been surprised when Mandsell answered, particularly as he had made several attempts to explain that he was not the person who had arranged to take the call.

The surprise of the day was to come. Just after the mid-morning break a girl came in with a note. Laura opened it and read:

Can you go out to lunch to-day? Something important.

H.H.T.

Laura recognized these initials as those of Mr Tomalin. Full of zeal for her task, she decided at once that he had something to contribute about Miss Faintley, so she scribbled at the bottom of the note:

Many thanks. See you at 12.15. L.M.

She felt contrite. Obviously she had misjudged Mr Tomalin. He must be much more intelligent and perceptive than she had supposed. He had tumbled to the reason for her presence at the school and was prepared to offer important information. It was in the friendliest spirit that she greeted him after morning school.

'Oh, yes,' said Tomalin, shortly, 'but it isn't me, of course. It's Bannister. I said I'd ask you on his behalf. He wouldn't ask you himself in case you refused.'

Laura laughed, and said she never refused an invitation to eat. Three minutes later the misanthropic Mr Bannister was blurting out that he thought they had better go to Hagford. 'If you don't mind using your car,' he concluded. 'That would give us nice time.'

'*I'm* going to drive, then.'

'Oh, yes. I can't, anyway. It's like this,' he went on, when they were in the car and Laura was on the straight road for Hagford, 'I've been thinking about that woman Faintley and I want to give you a bit of advice, if you wouldn't think it cheek. Anyway, I felt I ought to warn you that she wasn't everything she seemed, not by a long chalk, either. Don't you go getting mixed up in her affairs. If the school stock has to be called for at Hagford station, you let somebody else call for it. I don't like to see a young girl taking risks, if you don't think it impudent to say so.'

'To begin with,' said Laura, 'I'm not my own idea of a young girl. But, be that as it may, I'm glad you've mentioned Miss Faintley and the parcels, because I had an idea that Miss Golightly was a bit diffident about my going and getting them. Actually it was rather nice, because of getting the time off from school. But what do you mean about taking risks? It was nothing to do with the school stock that Miss Faintley got killed.'

'Not to do with the school stock, no. But that wasn't the only thing she used to collect from Hagford Junction, you know. Turn left here. We'll go to the Crown. It's quite the best pub for lunch. I do hope you don't mind my inviting you out? I know you usually go with some of the women, which would naturally be more fun for you than this, but I didn't see any chance of talking to you at school. Well, here we are. It's all right to park outside.'

He took her into the saloon bar, and asked what she would drink.

'Mustn't be long,' said Laura, accepting sherry and glancing at her watch.

'It's all right. I booked a table on the off-chance that you would come, and Williams knows me. He'll see we get served nice and quickly. Now, look, this woman Faintley. I happen to know that she used the school parcels to cover another activity. I found it out by accident one day last term. A boy, fooling about while I was out of the room, got a jab with the point of a compass. It was so near the eye that Miss Golightly thought I'd better take him over to the hospital. On the way back by myself I saw Miss Faintley get out of her car and go with a parcel into a small shop. She didn't see me because I was behind her. I glanced into the shop as I passed it, and there was rather an unsavoury specimen behind the counter who was shelling her out some pound notes. Just as I glanced in he leaned across and gave her a ringing slap in the face. I didn't like that much, so I charged in and bellowed at him. But Faintley wasn't grateful. She said, "Don't interfere in family disagreements," but I said I didn't like to see women knocked about, even by their fathers. The chap turned suddenly very civil and said he did not often lose his temper with his niece, and he asked me whether I was a master at the school, and Miss Faintley told him I was, and invited me to go back with her in her car. As we were driving back she begged me not to mention that she had called to see her uncle, as she was out on school business and had had no business to have gone into the shop at all. I promised, of course, but I wasn't satisfied. I couldn't believe that he *was* her uncle, so, on the quiet, I made a few inquiries. The police superintendent is by way of being a pal of mine. He said the police suspected this shopkeeper . . .

Tomson his name is . . . of being a burglars' fence. It didn't square at all with what I knew about Faintley, and then, of course, she got murdered. As soon as I heard about that, I went to the police station and told them about this parcel and pound note business, but it was too late to do any good, of course. Still, when I found that you'd been sent to the station for the goods, I thought it was very unfair if you got let in, unknowingly, for anything fishy, so I thought I'd like to tip you off, so to speak. Any more sherry? Then perhaps we'd better go in.'

Laura enjoyed the lunch. It became more and more apparent that Mr Bannister, far from being a woman-hater, was simply and solely terrified of the whole sex. He was obviously chivalrous and kindhearted, and she began to like him and to hope that her suspicions about him were unfounded.

'I suppose,' he said hesitantly, when they were on their way back to school, 'you wouldn't care to come out with me on Saturday? We could walk over the hills, if you liked, and have tea somewhere, and perhaps have a bit of dinner afterwards and do a film. There's quite a decent one this week over at Dashford Mills, and the kids don't get out as far as that on a Saturday night, so there wouldn't be any comment.'

'I know a scheme worth two of that,' said Laura, suddenly inspired. 'You come and stay with us for the weekend. You'll like my boss, I know.'

'Your boss?'

'Yes. Miss Faintley was not all she seemed, and I'm not, either. Will you come to Wandles Parva and make the acquaintance of Mrs Lestrange Bradley?'

Before she drove back that evening she telephoned her employer: 'Bringing home suspect number one. Kill the fatted calf. He stood me a very good lunch to-day in Hagford. There's something up his sleeve which I expect you'll find some way of shaking down. He told me a most unlikely yarn about himself and Faintley. I'm dying to know the truth about him. It's Bannister.'

'Mr Bannister?' Mrs Bradley replied. 'You have indeed done well. Do you remember that I took Mark to visit Lascaux?'

'Where the ferns grow?'

'No, not ferns, but many more horses than the four horsemen of the Apocalypse ever dreamed of. Mr Bannister is well known at Lascaux. How lucky for me that I took Mark along with me that day!'

'Kind hearts are more than coronets,' said Laura ironically. She still did not believe that Mrs Bradley had had no ulterior motive in taking Mark to France.

CHAPTER TEN

MRS CROCODILE

*

'. . . with gently-smiling jaws.'

LEWIS CARROLL – *Alice in Wonderland*

MRS BRADLEY had spent the day in the way which she had outlined to Laura, but she was back at the Stone House in the little Hampshire village of Wandles Parva before Laura drove home from school, and received the telephone message immediately upon her arrival.

'First things first,' she said, after Laura had been up to bath and change before dinner. 'We have Madras curry and Henri's peculiarly luscious chutney.'

'And those pancake things that always remind me of bits of fried fur coat?'

'And those.'

'Oh, good! I'm famished. And how did you get on in Kindleford to-day?'

'Unexpectedly well.'

Mrs Bradley had indeed gained rather more information in Kindleford than she had considered possible. She had gone straight to Detective-Inspector Darling for news of the statue.

'We took it to bits and found nothing inside but a fern leaf. That seems to prove that Tomson wasn't lying to us, but it doesn't help us over Mandsell's *flat* parcel.'

'Interesting. *Which* fern leaf?' Mrs Bradley had inquired.

'How should I know? I know nothing at all about ferns.'

'A great pity. May I see it?'

Carefully and painstakingly mounted by a young constable who had a gift for handling delicate fragments which enabled him, later, as a detective-superintendent, to solve the notorious mystery of the blue butterfly murders, the fern leaf had been produced for her inspection.

'*Asplenium Ceterach* – the Scaly Spleenwort, Inspector.'

'Really, ma'am? You're an authority, then, on ferns?'

'No, no. But I have a reasonably good visual and verbal memory. I recognize this specimen because it is exactly like one I saw in a glass case in the house at Cromlech.'

'The house outside which Miss Faintley was found murdered? That's remarkably interesting, ma'am. But as we already know that Miss Faintley was connected with the parcels, I don't see quite how it helps us.'

'It tails in with a theory I have formed, Inspector. The fact that two men thought it necessary to remove the case of mounted and labelled ferns from Cromlech Down House, coupled with the very different type of package which Mr Mandsell collected from Hagford when Miss Faintley was prevented from going to get it, causes me to think that the fern in the statue may possibly form part of a code.'

'A code, ma'am? Yes, we had something of the same idea ourselves, but – well, I don't know, I'm sure.'

'Well, what else can you suggest?'

'Nothing, until we get the whole truth out of Tomson, and that isn't going to be easy. Though, of course, he did confess he broke a statue Miss Faintley had once collected.'

'*Asplenium Ceterach* – the Scaly Spleenwort,' repeated Mrs Bradley thoughtfully. She took out a pocket mirror, glanced at her reflexion, and chuckled. 'Extraordinary. Do you suppose it was the same parcel as the one which the zealous station official refused to allow Miss Menzies to collect? I should like to believe that. Although he did not let her have it, for us the result is the same as though he had yielded it up, it seems to me.'

'A substitute parcel, ma'am? No, I hadn't thought of that!'

'Miss Menzies has very sharp eyes. The parcel she saw was a flat one. You think that your brains have not received their due meed of appreciation from the enemy? I feel certain, you know, that they have, and it seems to me that the common-sense thing for the gang to do would be to make certain that the police were not presented with the right bit of the code. What is more, their leader has a grim sense of humour. The Scaly Spleenwort! Quite the rasp-berry, Inspector, in other words.'

'Are you going to have a talk with Tomson, ma'am?' asked Darling, after a pause during which he had appeared to cogitate.

'It can do no harm. In fact, I must do it, although not much is likely to come of it. Tomson, I daresay, has been carefully briefed. But first I'll go and see your Mr Mandsell.'

Mandsell was out when she called. Mrs Deaks suggested that she should wait.

'He won't be long, madam. Just gone to look up the library, so he said. The trouble with him is that he goes to look up one thing and finishes up with half a dozen things quite different – or so he says. Still, he ain't a mite of trouble, even if he don't pay up, but I think his intentions is honourable, and I wouldn't turn him into the street no more, whatever my husband may say. If you'd seen the way that poor boy came in sopping wet the time we give him his notice – well, you wouldn't treat a dog like it, let alone a young fellow what is on his beam ends and acts to you like a gentleman, not for Deaks nor for nobody do I do it, not never no more.'

'You're a kind woman, Mrs Deaks. It is not everybody who would feel like that. He is greatly in your debt.'

'Well, not so much as you might think,' replied the literal-minded landlady. 'He give me four pound the next day, although goodness' knows where he got it, and then he've got twenty pounds since then for some story or other he wrote, so I'm very pleased to think we should keep him on, for anybody less trouble as a lodger you couldn't find, and that I'll maintain to my dying day.'

'In other words, you like Mr Mandsell. Does he have friends here to visit him?'

'No, he don't. Not one extra meal have I ever been asked to provide, and that's something in these days. Mrs Froud, down the street, she's got two young ladies in her top front, shorthand typists – one at Mr Fuller's, the lawyers', and the other at the shoe factory office – and they're always having people in to tea. She charges, of course, but that don't make up for the trouble, and dirty shoes in and out, and the getting ready and the washing-up and that, not to speak of all hours and a lot of stale tobacco smoke and the wear and tear on the carpet and furniture, and face powder over the dressing-table and cigarette ash on the floor. I tell her to tell 'em to go, but it ain't all that easy to get double money with two young ladies sharing, and they *will* sometimes do a hand's turn for theirselves, which is more than my young gentleman does. Still, I'd rather have a man. It don't seem natural in a woman of my years to wait on bits of girls.'

'I suppose a young man can be a trial in other ways, though. Late hours, perhaps one drink too many, staying away the night without letting you know – '

'Not Mr Mandsell,' said Mrs Deaks decisively. 'He don't understand what housework is, and he *will* climb in through the window instead of coming in at the door – but that's usually because, being a writer, he's an absent-minded young gentleman and often forgets his key. But, apart from that, and the money not always being there when it oughter – though I *will* say it always turns up later, and sometimes, p'raps, a bunch of flowers or some sweets with it as well if he's kept me waiting more than a couple of weeks – well, I haven't no complaints. Of course, he do make a proper old mess in the bathroom and no idea of cleaning the bath down after hisself, but I suppose that comes of being a gentleman born.'

Mrs Bradley could obtain no more precise information and knew better than to fish with too many leading questions. She had gathered what she wanted, however. It seemed unreasonable to suppose that Mandsell had had any previous connexion with Miss Faintley or her murderers.

He was chronically hard up, kept reasonable hours, and made no uncharted voyages into the world at large. Mentally Mrs Bradley dismissed him from the case.

Left to herself, she settled down in the stuffy little parlour to wait for him, and then, finding the atmosphere oppressive, she ventured to open the window. Shortly afterwards Mandsell, who once again had forgotten his key, climbed through it to meet her black-eyed, gimlet gaze.

'Oh, hullo,' he said. 'Awfully sorry. Didn't know anyone was here. I usually get in through the kitchen. This one isn't very often open.'

He began to retreat towards the door but Mrs Bradley stopped him.

'I represent the Home Office,' she said. 'I take it that you are Geoffrey Mandsell. I should very much like a short talk with you, Mr Mandsell.'

'Oh, I say, though! I've had the police already! You don't mean you're connected with Miss Faintley?'

'In a sense, yes, and I may add that the police know I'm here. There are one or two points, Mr Mandsell, which I think we can resolve right away, if you will co-operate with me.'

'Oh, I don't think so, you know. The police have cleaned me right out. If you've heard what I've told them, you've heard all.'

'So you suppose. Sit down and answer my questions.' Mandsell hesitated. 'You have nothing to fear,' she added, 'have you?'

'No, of course, I haven't – only – well, I did take five pounds off that rat of a little shopkeeper. I was completely broke, and I knew I had money coming to me, so – '

'Where did the money come from? Where had he kept it?'

'Where? Oh, I see. He got it out of the till.'

'Which day of the week was it?'

'Friday.'

'And the Thursday had been early closing day?'

'Yes. Yes, it had.'

'With only half a day's takings and . . . at what time did you get to him on the Friday?'

'At about four, I suppose. Before he closed, anyhow.'

'With only half a day on Thursday and between six and seven hours of shopping time on Friday, then, would you really have expected, in a shop of that kind, the man to have been able to take five pounds out of the till?'

'Now you come to put it like that, well, I suppose I wouldn't have expected it.'

'And now that you realize it was an unusual thing to have happened, are you still certain that there is nothing else you can tell me?'

'I can tell you one thing,' said Mandsell vigorously. 'I wish I'd never touched that beastly parcel!'

'It may be very helpful to the police that you did. Tell me, Mr Mandsell, what really induced you to call for that parcel at all?'

'I don't know. The Inspector wanted me to tell him that. It was just a sudden idea.'

'But why, Mr Mandsell? You must have known it was none of your business.'

Mandsell looked unhappy. He racked his brains. This extraordinary old lady obviously was determined to have an answer, and the answer, her black eyes and beaky little mouth suggested, had better be a satisfactory one. She cackled with a suddenness and a harshness that made him start.

'I – I beg your pardon?' he stammered. She did not answer. In a terrifying way she waited. He was mesmerized into replying to her question. 'I went because, I suppose, it was something to do. I was a bit at a loose end, that was all.'

'You went, in response to an unexpected summons from an unknown woman, knowing quite well that she had mistaken you for someone else, to a railway station five miles distant from your lodgings, to pick up and deliver a parcel (of whose nature and contents you were unaware) to a seedy little man in a back-street shop in this town? I still ask why you did it, Mr Mandsell.'

Mandsell felt still more unhappy, and looked so.

'I've really no idea,' he replied. 'I mean that. I don't know why I went. It was just one of those things.'

'And as a result of "one of those things" a woman has been murdered.'

'Oh, but I couldn't possibly have thought that that was going to happen!'

'You didn't think at all. Come, now, Mr Mandsell, tell me why you did it.'

This persistence had its effect.

'I was on my beam ends. I was pretty desperate. I'd been turned out of my digs and . . . well, to tell you the truth . . . I thought there might be something in it for me, even if it was only a bob to buy some grub.'

'You were as badly off as that?'

'At that moment, yes, I was. Of course, I *shall* be all right when my book comes out, but meanwhile it's fairly sticky going. Still, I've sold a short story. That's something.'

'Yes, yes, so it is. Mr Mandsell, you will have gathered that the police and I are extremely interested in these five one-pound notes which shopkeeper Tomson gave you.'

'Oh, Lord! You don't think they're dud ones? I've paid four of them over to my landlady!'

'Have you any idea what she did with them?'

'Yes, of course. They're in the teapot.'

'Still?'

'Oh, yes. She won't put money in the Savings Bank because of the Income Tax, and she won't buy National Savings Certificates because she thinks they're a nuisance to cash, and she's saving up to visit her daughter in Canada.'

'Banking account?'

'Not she. Says the young gents behind the counter look down on the likes of her. I told her that was nonsense. The trouble is, she's almost illiterate, I think, and it gives her a rather vast sense of inferiority.'

'I should like to see those notes.'

Mandsell looked dubious.

'You know what those sort of people are like about money.'

'She must either show them to me or take them to the police station. They may be very important evidence against Tomson if he's been up to anything shady.'

'Well, honestly, *I* daren't ask her to produce them! My standing in this house isn't all that hot, you know, and if Deaks begins thinking that I've paid my bill with dud notes . . .'

But Mrs Deaks, under the influence of Mrs Bradley's beautiful voice and tactful handling, was not at all averse to displaying the notes.

'Thing is, dear,' she said confidentially, 'as I didn't want to upset my 'usband *nor* Mr Mandsell, but it seemed sort of funny to me, if you take my meaning, him being on his beam-ends one minute and flashin' out four pounds the next, so I kep' 'em separate. Here they is, look, with a rubber band around 'em.'

Mrs Bradley was not an expert in detecting forgeries, but an enthusiastic Scotland Yard officer had once spent an entire morning in pointing out to her the slight errors by which even the cleverest forgers are tripped up. The most minute scrutiny of the four notes through her small but powerful magnifying glass failed to reveal any of the discrepancies she had been instructed to look for, however. She compared minutely each of the four notes with one from her own purse, but was compelled to conclude either that the forger had been a master of his trade, or else that the four notes were genuine. There was only one interesting feature. On three out of the four notes were traces of some blotchy outlines, and these were particularly clear on one, where they happened to come on the half-crown-sized white circle on the back.

She took from a small leather case some minute surgical forceps and very gingerly scratched at the marks. Memory, aided by the powerful magnifying glass, began to stir. She saw the darkish walls of the Lateral Passage at Lascaux, its sandy floor and the dust at the foot of its walls. She remembered that here alone, in this spine-chilling underground temple of primitive man with its terrifying suggestion of art come alive through the 'monstrous power of witchcraft', could be detected the slight atmosphere of damp sufficient for the growth of a form of prehistoric mould, 'an archaic fungus,' says Alan Houghton Brodrick in his *Lascaux.*

It was not often that Mrs Bradley felt the tingling excitement in which half Laura Menzies' young, lusty life was lived, but she felt it now.

Monsieur Banneestaire! And Monsieur Bannister had been to Lascaux! Was there ... could there be ... any connexion?

'This is valuable evidence,' she said impressively. 'Will you exchange these four notes for four I will give you, or will you take them straight to the police station?'

'I don't want nothing to do with the police,' said Mrs Deaks slowly. 'If so be as you'll agree to mark the notes you gives me with Deaks' undelyable pencil, and if so be as you agrees to 'ave Mr Mandsell in as a witness to me giving you up his notes in exchange for yours, well, I don't mind changing 'em. If yours is duds and those is duds, well, I shan't be no worse off,' she concluded with her class's deep philosophy.

Mandsell was called into the kitchen, and the notes were marked and exchanged.

'Now for the villainous Tomson,' said Mrs Bradley.

'Yes,' said Mandsell, brightening. '*Yes*! I wouldn't at all mind confronting that bloke. I'll give him my I.O.U. That ought to settle his hash, one way or the other. I mean, he'll either have to come clean about the parcel or lose his money.'

'No, no. You must leave the negotiations to me.'

Upon this understanding they sought out Tomson. He did not seem pleased to see them, and asked them, in surly and unwilling fashion, what he could have the honour of showing them.

'Faintley-coloured materials,' Mrs Bradley replied.

'Pastel shades, madam? Those on the shelves are all I have in stock. Would anything of that kind suit you?'

'No, no. I require curtains the colour of blood.'

'Blood, madam? I don't know that I – '

'No? A great pity. Have you never heard of blood-coloured curtains? Faintley-coloured and blood-coloured are quite the rage nowadays, you know. Oh, and my second cousin here believes that he owes you five pounds. Can you remember the transaction, I wonder?'

'What's your game?' demanded Tomson, suddenly abandoning any pretence of being the anxious shopkeeper and becoming, with one short question, the anxious petty criminal. 'You never come here to buy curtains!'

'I wonder how you know that? Can you possibly have a guilty conscience, my poor man? Never mind. We have come to return the five pounds which you so kindly lent to my ward here. May we have a receipt?'

'You can go to hell!' said Tomson, snarling. 'Get out of my shop, the pair of you! I don't know nothing about any five pounds, but I knows the confidence trick when I sees it!'

Mrs Bradley slowly shook her head and Tomson was suddenly reminded of a cobra he had seen in his youth on a trip to the London Zoo.

'It won't do at all,' she said gently. 'What species of fern did you find in the statue you broke?'

This question really frightened Tomson.

'I didn't find nothing in the statue,' he asserted. 'And I never broke it! It was broke when it landed up 'ere!'

'I think you found *Ophioglossum Vulgatum* – in other words, the adder's-tongue fern,' she said. 'And the police think you broke the statue deliberately and have confessed as much.'

'Adder's-tongue?' He licked his lips, his apprehension obviously increasing. 'What do you mean ... adder's-tongue? There wasn't nothing in it, I tell you! And I 'ave *not* said I broke the statue, because I never!'

'You have been warned,' pronounced Mrs Bradley,

solemnly. 'Come, dear fellow,' she added to Mandsell. 'This man is determined that nothing I can do shall save him.'

'I say, you scared him all right,' said Mandsell, when they were out of the shop. 'What exactly was all that in aid of?'

'Time will show, child. I wonder, however, that Tomson was left in peace when once he had allowed his curiosity to overcome him and had broken that statue. In fact, the only explanation . . . Yes, I think I see.'

'The thing I got from Hagford wasn't a statue, you know.'

'I do know, and thereby hangs a useful bit of evidence.'

'As how?'

'As nothing. Children should be seen and not heard, and most of their questions studiously although not unkindly ignored,' replied Mrs Bradley serenely. 'However, you leave the court without a stain on your character.'

'But nobody ever does who's been brought to court, you know.'

'I do know. But never mind. Better a live donkey than a dead lion.'

'I don't agree at all. I'd willingly die if I could die a lion instead of a donkey.'

'Some are born great, others achieve greatness – '

'I say, I wonder if some day you'd read a bit of my stuff? I mean, I don't think it's all that bad.'

'I shall be honoured.'

'You're pulling my leg.'

'Which is not my wont. I am unalterably serious-minded. I wonder whether there was a fern in *your* parcel, too?'

'What makes you think there might have been?'

'The answer to that is only for the police, and I don't know enough yet to confide in them.'

They parted at Mrs Deaks' house and the smooth car pulled up to take Mrs Bradley home. She leered kindly at Mandsell out of the near-side window, and reached Wandles Parva somewhat ahead of Laura, who brought with her the shy Mr Bannister.

'Ah!' said Mrs Bradley, peering at him as though he

were some dubious piece of meat which she suspected of being horse-flesh. 'What have we here?'

'This is Mr Bannister,' said Laura. 'Maths and all that, and took me out to lunch, you know. I phoned you.'

Mrs Bradley gazed snake-like upon Bannister, a proceeding which did not appear to disconcert him. In fact, her extraordinary appearance, clad as she was in cherry-red and faint purple, gave him confidence. He stretched out a flexible hand.

'This is great,' he said sincerely. 'I've always wanted to meet you.'

'Clever boy!' said Laura, returning Mrs Bradley's basilisk gaze with an impudent smile. 'When do we eat, O Egypt?'

The meal was a great success. Bannister proved to be an authority upon French cooking and was personally introduced to Henri, who rated him, forthwith, as the enviable possessor of an intelligence unusual and profound, with a knowledge of the French tongue unsurpassed even by Frenchmen.

'He is still English,' said Henri's wife Celestine, with a scowl (this in the privacy of the kitchen quarters), 'and it is well understood that all the English are barbarians.'

'But Madame is English, too!'

'Madame is not of this world,' said Celestine austerely. 'She is of another state of being. One cannot doubt it.'

'Nevertheless, this gentleman understands that I am a cook in a thousand, and has said so in beautiful French. A cook in a thousand! Remember that!'

'Fish-fry in heaven! And who is to pay?'

'The English Government,' said Henri, gurgling with laughter. Celestine tossed her head and picked up the tray of coffee. She affected to despise her spouse, but would have died for him. 'They are here a nation of the Welfare State,' Henri added. 'The poor have inherited the earth.'

'Blasphemy!' said Celestine sourly. She took in the coffee and set it down gently on a table at Mrs Bradley's right elbow. 'Madame is served!'

'And, in return, will give you a reliable recipe for poisoning Henri,' said her employer. Celestine tossed her head, as usual.

'Although a pig and a louse, he is still the husband my good parents found for me,' she said austerely. 'The good offices of *madame* are wasted on such as he!'

'Is she really such a tartar?' asked Bannister, who found himself at home in the household. Laura laughed.

'You'd be surprised,' she said. 'Now, Mrs Croc, let's pump him.'

Mrs Bradley regarded Bannister benevolently. She saw a tall, angular, dark-faced man, obviously shy but with honest eyes and a mouth which she thought could be grim.

'I hope you won't need to pump me,' he said. 'What about?'

'About the late Faintley, of course,' said Laura encouragingly. 'You can't tell us too much about her.'

'As for that,' said Bannister. He stopped, and looked to Mrs Bradley for guidance. 'As for that,' he repeated, 'well, I didn't really *know* much about her.'

'Perhaps not, but you were good enough to warn my secretary, Laura here, against picking up parcels at Hagford railway junction,' Mrs Bradley observed.

'I know,' said Bannister. 'The point is that . . . oh, well, I expect Miss Menzies has told you.'

'Whatever Miss Menzies has told me would be more valuable if I could have it at first hand . . . and that is all you can do to help us?' Mrs Bradley added, when Bannister had repeated his story of having seen Miss Faintley enter Tomson's shop, and of what he had witnessed there.

'I think so,' he replied, but he seemed uncertain.

'Then, in that case,' said Mrs Bradley, 'let us change the subject of conversation.' Bannister looked surprised at the abrupt alteration in her tone. 'Tell us about your potholing, and what you think of the prehistoric cave-paintings at Lascaux,' she suggested.

'Lascaux? . . . Oh, I suppose that young devil Street told you. He *said* he'd spent part of his holidays at Miss Menzies' hotel, and I knew from the papers that Miss Menzies had found Miss Faintley's body.' He stopped short; then he added, 'But you mean something deeper than that.'

'I've been to Lascaux myself,' Mrs Bradley assured him. 'You are remembered in the district.'

Bannister grimaced, but made no comment. Mrs Bradley pressed the point by remaining absolutely silent and nodding her head very slowly, as though she had discovered something which gave her satisfaction. Bannister suddenly laughed.

'I'm awfully sorry, but I've been tested for nerves, you know. The Gestapo technique was, if I may say so, bloodily more effective than yours. Still, I'll give this much away: Faintley, whether innocently or not, was mixed up with something no good, but it wasn't political, exactly. I'm pretty certain about that. I know all the symptoms, I think. And now . . . why did you ask me to come here?'

Mrs Bradley told him of Mandsell's telephone call, and Laura added:

'So far as we know, you and Mr Trench were the only men members of the staff who didn't turn up at all at that end-of-term dance. The man who had to answer the telephone call that night walked away in front of Mandsell, he was either you or Trench. I don't think it was you because . . . well, because I just don't think it was. Have you an alibi, by the way?'

'As a matter of fact, I suppose I have. I was fiddling about with my landlady's television set most of the evening. You could check that if you wanted to. She and her husband were with me most of the time, and once I'd got home from school I didn't go out any more until almost ten. I went down to the *Lion* then for a beer, and stayed until closing time.'

'Before which the telephone call must have been made. That brings us to Mr Trench, then. What sort of man is he? I've met him in the staff-room, of course, but I haven't gathered yet what he's really like.'

'And you won't. He's a bit of an *homme incompris*. Nobody

knows much about him. He's all right at his job, but his wife's a chronic invalid and he seems to spend most of his time out of school in waiting upon the sick-bed. Trouble is, I gather, that he married above him, and hasn't ever been able to live it down. I don't think the wife is bitchy, but now she's ill he feels he must try to make up to her for a disappointing sort of life. Odd bloke. Might be quite decent but for this rotten fixation.'

'A man, in fact, who would be glad of a little extra dough?'

'I should say so. Chickens and invalid diet and fairly exotic fruit and flowers, and a hefty library subscription, and taxi fares if she ventures out, can run into money, of course, and nothing's too good for the lady – or so we gather. None of us has been permitted to meet her, by the way. Her blue blood, apart from her illness, has to be respected, and I imagine that our staff don't measure up.'

'Oh, I *see*!' said Laura, enlightened. 'Do you think he's *really* an impartial witness?' she asked Mrs Bradley next morning before Bannister had appeared downstairs for breakfast.

'I think he's sufficiently impartial for our purposes,' Mrs Bradley replied, 'but there is one point on which he is misinformed, I think.'

'About Trench?'

'About *Mrs* Trench . . . but we shall see! And, of course, he made a splendid Freudian slip of the tongue, did he not?'

As soon as breakfast was over Mrs Bradley sent Bannister and Laura out for a long walk and caused George to drive into Kindleford, where she herself picked up Mandsell, and, luring him from his new novel with the promise of luxurious food and the car to return him to the Deaks' house immediately dinner was over, took him back with her to the Stone House at Wandles Parva.

'There is only one thing I am going to ask you to do,' she told him before they arrived. 'I am entertaining a guest who might or might not be the individual you saw walking away from the telephone-box in Park Road.'

'And you want to find out whether there's any chance I can say yea or nay, I suppose? Well, there's *not* much chance, I ought to tell you. You see, it was pretty gloomy, what with the evening and the rain and all that, and I only saw his back view, and not very close to, either. Still, I'll do my best, of course. But if I'm not absolutely sure (and I don't see how I can be) I'm not going to let the bloke in for trouble with the police.'

'Fair enough, child, and I shall give you no prompting. I think myself that it is very unlikely that you will be able to commit yourself to any definite statement on the matter, but I feel compelled to try the experiment. Incidentally, this man is not suspected of having been Miss Faintley's murderer. You need have no scruples about meeting him.'

'I'm disappointed to hear that! I've never met a murderer except in wax, at Madame Tussaud's, and I'd rather like to!'

They got back to the Stone House in plenty of time for lunch, and by the time the poverty-stricken young author had finished his meal and remembered that, on the same luxurious lines, there was dinner still to come, there was almost nothing he would not have done for his hostess. He eyed Bannister with cautious curiosity, and, as soon as opportunity offered (which was when Laura took Bannister off to look at Mrs Bradley's pigs . . . her Oxfordshire nephew having insisted upon presenting her that year with a litter of Large Whites so that she need not eat ewe mutton unless she wanted to) he shook his head and said:

'It's all right. I'm absolutely positive. He's far too tall. The fellow I saw was about my own height . . . certainly not more. Besides, this man's got an entirely different walk. Even with his blazer collar turned up, as he's got it now, and slouching along with his head forward and his hands in his pockets, he doesn't look in the least like my bloke, who was walking with his coat collar up, too, because of the rain.'

'You are positive?'

'Positive. You see, my job makes me sort of register

things, especially sensory impressions. Oh, no, this isn't the telephone chap. It couldn't possibly be. I'm certain enough to take my oath on it.'

'Pass, Mr Bannister, and all's well . . . so far,' said Mrs Bradley to Laura, while the two men were having their after-dinner port before Mandsell was taken back to Kindleford.

'So far?' echoed Laura.

'Yes. I am inclined to share his view that the activities of the Faintley gang are not political, and it certainly seems, from Mr Mandsell's evidence, that it was not Mr Bannister who had agreed to take that call. All the same . . . ' she paused and meditated.

'What was that crack of yours about a Freudian error?' Laura inquired, at the end of a dutiful period of silence.

'He called Mr Trench an *homme incompris*. But that is what he himself had to be during the war. He was known to the guardians at Lascaux, and the Germans undoubtedly knew of him. So much I think he made clear. When all this is over, we must ask him for the story of his adventures. They were probably fantastic.'

'And a man like that settles down to teach elementary mathematics to kids,' said Laura. 'Not bad at it, either, let me tell you.'

'And how good a teacher is Mr Trench?'

'You'd better ask him,' said Laura. 'I don't know the first thing about the woodwork and metalwork centre.'

'Mr Bannister must be our informant, then. I want to know as much about Mr Trench as he will tell you.'

'Bannister?'

'Mr Bannister in person. You had better warn him that anything he says may be taken down and used in evidence.'

'You don't want *me*, then. You want Vardon, I should say.'

'Mr Bannister would not like to confide in Detective-Inspector Vardon. I suggest that he would like to confide in one of us, and, of the two of us, you would be the more likely to gain the truth from him.'

'So that I can spill it to you?'

'Mr Bannister will be more than agreeable to that course of procedure, dear child. He is anxious to confide in someone.'

'All right, but I shall ask him first, you know, whether that's really what he wants.'

'To use your own fearsome idiom, I couldn't agree more.'

'Oh, you couldn't?' said Laura, uneasily. She was still inexperienced enough to share young Mark Street's schoolboy instinct that when the grown-ups agreed with you you had better watch out. Laura had not quite outgrown her terror of the goblins. Demoniacal possession, she sensed (wrongly) to be the prerogative of the adult world. Mrs Bradley realized this, and cackled. Laura looked reproachful.

'Look here,' she said to Bannister, when they were together in the garden after Mandsell had gone home that night, 'Mrs Croc. has her optics on you. What was all that about you and the caves at Lascaux? And the Gestapo, and so forth?'

'Yes,' replied Bannister absently. 'I know what she meant. I was in the Resistance, of course. One of the lucky ones, on the whole. Parachuted in, and my mother was French, so I had the gab and knew the country. We used to hide blokes . . . our own and others. Not in Lascaux itself . . . it was too well known . . . but there are lots of caves in that part of France. We winkled chaps out of occupied France and sometimes out of Italy, and smuggled them away through . . . well, I'd better not tell you. It might be needed again, and the higher the fewer, so to speak.'

'Well, what about Trench? I've been told to pump you about him. What can you tell us?'

'Nothing at all. He wasn't mixed up with my push, if that's what you mean. I met him for the first time on the school staff. Why? What has he got to do with it? . . . No, I won't ask you that. I see the issue quite plainly. Your boss thinks that either Trench or I did in Faintley because one of us was scheduled to take that telephone call, and we were the only men not at school that night. I don't see Trench as a murderer. I'm sure he is more or less all right in himself. Trouble is, he's Red, and, not only that, but like lots of chaps who happen to be under the weather, he's become fanatical – you know, agin the Government, and all that – but that doesn't mean he'd do any harm. Of course, it's obvious that, saddled with that wife of his who's always being ill, he must be pretty badly stuck for money, and it's true he never seems to be all that short. Beyond that, I can tell you nothing.'

'But you don't think he'd commit murder?'

'It depends upon what you call murder, you know. After all, we murder people when we hang them.'

Laura had heard this view expressed by her employer.

'That's what Mrs Croc. says,' she answered. 'Well, we'd better go in. It's getting a bit chilly out here.'

'Ah, Mr Bannister,' said Mrs Bradley, when they re-entered the Stone House. 'I've been thinking about the caves at Lascaux while you two have been out in the garden. Why it is that I seemed to sense a difference between the atmosphere of the Lateral Passage and that of, say, the Hall or the Nave?'

'Oh, that's easy,' replied Bannister, frankly and immediately. 'I expect you mean that the Lateral Passage is slightly damp in places. There's a peculiar kind of ancient mould or fungus growing on parts of the walls.'

Early on the following morning Mrs Bradley telephoned to Detective-Inspector Darling that she proposed to interview Mr and Mrs Trench.

CHAPTER ELEVEN

MR TRENCH

*

'. . . by fines so heavy that for some time afterwards
a Castillian would take off his hat at sight of a piece
of gold.'

HELEN SIMPSON – *The Spanish Marriage*

EARLY on Monday morning Mrs Bradley went in person
to Miss Golightly to ask for Trench's address. Miss Golightly
had to be persuaded into giving it. She could not imagine,
she said, that Mr Trench was involved in Miss Faintley's
affairs. He was a most reliable and unassuming man.

Mrs Bradley explained that if anyone on the school staff
was involved it had seemed likely that it must be either Mr
Trench or Mr Bannister. She added that she had had Mr
Bannister to her country house for the week-end and had
questioned him. Now it was Mr Trench's turn, and she
proposed to interview not only Mr Trench but his wife.

'I understand that she is an invalid,' she added, 'but as
I am a doctor you need have no fear that I shall upset her
if she really appears to be ill. And do you mind not telling
Mr Trench that I am going to see his wife? What is she
like, by the way?'

'I have never met her,' Miss Golightly replied. Then she
gave the address, and added, 'How I do hate all this! It
seems dreadful to go behind the backs of my staff. I've
never done it before.'

'You haven't had one of them murdered before,' Mrs
Bradley pointed out in mild tones. 'By the way, I have sent
Miss Menzies to you this morning, but her fortnight was
up on Friday, and I should be grateful if you would release

her before the end of the week. I want to get back to Crom-lech. There is not a great deal more that we can do here at present, when once I have interviewed Mr and Mrs Trench.'

'I see. Perhaps you would like me to release Miss Menzies after the end of to-morrow.'

'If that would not inconvenience you too much.'

'No, no. I think that will be all right. The Office have now promised me a Supply. I will ring them immediately.'

Laura, informed during the course of the morning of her impending release, was duly grateful.

'I don't mean I haven't enjoyed it,' she said. 'It's been fun in a way. But . . . well, you know how it is!'

Miss Golightly agreed that she did, and added thought-fully that she imagined nature study and botany were not favourite subjects with Miss Menzies. Miss Menzies, grin-ning wryly, replied that she preferred English, and added Miss Topas' famous rider to text-books on botany that she knew only one Natural Order – that of Fools! Miss Topas, she added, was a genius, and had lectured at College in history.

So Laura and her headmistress parted on terms of mutual and undisguised friendship and relief, and Laura, at lunch-time, broke the news to Miss Cardillon that on Wednesday the school was due for a change on the staff.

Mrs Bradley, meanwhile, had parked her car some distance from Trench's house, and had gone on foot to interview his wife.

The door was answered by a middle-aged woman wear-ing a soiled dressing-gown. Her hair was untidy and last night's make-up was still on her face. Her eyes were hooded under deeply purple lids and her speech was thick and slurred.

'Yes, dear?' she asked, holding on to the door for support. 'If it's Trench, he isn't at home.'

'It isn't your husband I want to see. It's you.'

She wondered, however, whether much was to be gained from a woman who was so obviously drunk. *In vino veritas*, no doubt, but that did not necessarily imply giving correct and intelligent answers which could help an inquiry into a case of wilful murder.

'Me? What about? I don't know you, do I? I don't remember meeting you before. But I get muddled, you know, dear. It's my head. You wouldn't believe the head-aches I get. Something cruel.'

She swayed a little.

'No, you haven't met me before,' Mrs Bradley assured her. 'I am connected with the police.'

'I haven't done nothing that I know of.' She looked alarmed, and straightened up a little. 'I've paid my way, so far as I remember. I may be D.,' she added, with a pathetic attempt at a propitiatory smile, 'but I've never been D. and D., dear, not to be a nuisance outside, that is. Unless I've forgot. I do forget things sometimes. I never had much of a memory, even as a girl at school.'

'School? Ah, yes. Your husband's a schoolmaster, I believe.'

'He doesn't schoolmaster it here,' said Mrs Trench aus-terely, with a dignity which was somewhat marred by a slight belch. 'Pardon. If we're going to talk about Boffin, you'd better come in. My neighbours is all ears, as you'd imagine.'

She led the way along a smelly passage into a littered room. Bread, cheese, a half-empty bottle of brandy, some unwashed cups, a piece of knitting, a novelette, a scattered pack of cards and a book on fortune-telling were on the table, and dust was thick on mantelpiece, sideboard and the wooden arms of chairs. The curtains were drawn across the windows and the electric light was on. Crumbs and cigarette ash covered most of the hearthrug, and a couple of empty brandy bottles were standing in the alcove next to the fire-place. The room was airless and stank of drink and stale tobacco.

'And now, what do you want?' demanded Mrs Trench in altered tones. 'Boffin didn't send you, did he?'

'I want some information about the late Miss Faintley,' said Mrs Bradley coolly. 'Did you and Mr Trench know her before she came to live in Kindleford?'

'Miss Faintley? Who's she?'

'She was a teacher at the school.'

'So he's been up to something! I guessed as much! Him and his N.U.T. Conferences! I thought as how they seemed to come round pretty often! Carrying on with the lady teachers, is he? I wonder how long *that's* been going on?'

'It is nothing of that kind, Mrs Trench. The police are inquiring into the circumstances under which Miss Faintley met her death, and we think your husband might be able to help a little.'

'Him?' The woman looked shocked. 'There's nothing like *that* about him! He wouldn't harm a fly! If the coppers have got suspicions of my husband they must be even bigger fools than I take them for!'

'They are not fools, Mrs Trench, and they do not suspect your husband of having committed a criminal act. Did you go away for a summer holiday this year?'

'No, I didn't. I stayed here in Kindleford, same as I always do. I haven't had a decent holiday, not since the war.' She wiped her eyes, and continued in maudlin accents: 'The war upset me properly. We wasn't here then; we was near London, and the bombing got on my nerves, and I haven't really ever got over it.'

'No, it was a bad time,' said Mrs Bradley, who had remained in London, mostly at a casualty clearing station, during the worst of the air-raids. 'Well, thank you for our little chat. I had better go now. Don't get up. I can see myself out.'

She went at once. No protestations followed her. The moment she reached the front door Mrs Trench reached for the brandy and slopped some into a glass, fumbled in her dressing-gown pocket for cigarettes, and, after four attempts, managed to light one.

Mrs Bradley returned to Kindleford school and decided not to wait until the children were dismissed before interviewing Trench. The discovery that Mrs Trench was an habitual inebriate sufficiently explained her husband's excuses for his absence from school functions. To these she could never accept an invitation, and probably (thought Mrs Bradley) the unfortunate man felt that it was better to be at home to make certain that she did not, in her drunken wilfulness, come to the school entertainments, and, by her conduct, betray the secret he had guarded so jealously for so long.

The trouble was that it seemed only too likely, in view of the amount of money her brandy-tippling must cost him, that Trench might have been tempted to augment his income by dabbling in the affairs of the fern experts, whatever those affairs might be. It seemed highly probable that he and Miss Faintley had been in collusion, even in partnership, over the delivery of the mysterious parcels, and that she had felt perfectly safe in advising him to be at the public telephone in Park Road to take an emergency call.

Miss Golightly seemed to extend a rather frigid hand when Mrs Bradley arrived at the school.

'Interview Mr Trench *here?*' she asked. 'I suppose, if you want to, you must. You had better talk to him down here in my room. I will look after his class while you see him. Let me see, now . . . oh, yes.' She pressed a buzzer at the side of her desk and a boy with a cow-lick and a large, solid girl appeared. 'Mr Trench in the woodwork centre,' she said. 'Ask him to get all tools put away, library books out, and to come to my room as soon as he can manage it. My compliments, as usual, of course. You go, Roberts. Marion, run across to the cookery centre and ask Miss Welling to spare me a moment if there is nothing in the ovens. If there is, tell her I will come over to her. My compliments, of course, as usual.'

There proved to be nothing in the ovens, as the class was having an extra laundry lesson as a punishment for having eaten sultanas instead of dropping the full quota into the boiled puddings, so Miss Welling shortly appeared. She was an alert young woman of about twenty-eight, full of grievances, and Mrs Bradley's presence did nothing to render her inarticulate.

'And if I've told Susie Jenkins *once* to go and wash her hands and face before she comes to class, I've told her a dozen times, Miss Golightly. After all, if we can't have personal hygiene in the cookery centre, where *can* we have it?'

'Send her to me,' said the headmistress, with (Mrs Bradley suspected) an inaudible but heartfelt groan.

'*And*, Miss Golightly, I'm sure Brown's are not sending me my full sugar. The staff are always complaining about no extra sugar for the stewed fruit ... If it's not Brown's, then the children eat it, and I *always* keep everything locked up, so I don't see how ...'

'Sugar for the stewed fruit is the business of the school meals service. The staff cannot expect to come on to the cookery centre for more, Miss Welling.'

'Well, they always have,' said Miss Welling, unanswerably, 'and they think I'm being mean about it, and it's most unpleasant, especially the men. They seem to think I'm *made* of sugar ... no, I don't mean *that*, exactly ...'

'I will put up a notice in the staff-room. And you had better go to Brown's yourself instead of sending girls. And now, Miss Welling, what I really wanted to see you about ... Oh, here is Mr Trench. Excuse me one moment. Ah, Mr Trench, Mrs Bradley, who is assisting the police in an inquiry into the circumstances of Miss Faintley's death, would be glad of a word with you. She thinks you may be able to help her. Miss Welling, if you will walk across to the woodwork centre with me, I will ...'

Her voice grew muffled and then faded, as she and Miss Welling went out. Mr Trench, a small, compactly-built man with greying hair and a weak chin, closed the door and looked inquiringly at Mrs Bradley.

'I've been to see your wife,' she said. His expression changed.

'Yes? She's – she's quite an invalid, I'm afraid.'

'Indeed? She seemed to know very little about Miss Faintley.'

'I shouldn't think she knew her at all. You will have

gathered that my wife had really no connexion with the school.'

'What was your connexion with Miss Faintley, Mr Trench?'

'I don't think I had much connexion with her. Our subjects did not overlap, and I –'

'And you were only able to take an occasional telephone message. That much I understand. What I do *not* understand is this extraordinary business of the parcels of ferns.'

'Ferns? Oh, but I had nothing to do with that.'

'With what?'

'Well, the parcels, you know. I know she used to collect them, and then, when she said would I go, and I rang her up ... or, rather, she rang *me* up ... well, she just wasn't there, do you see?'

'I know all this, Mr Trench. Miss Faintley is dead. She was murdered. We have to find her murderer. You agree?'

'Of course I do. But I can't help you. What happened was this: Faintley ... Miss Faintley, I should say ... asked me to go to the public telephone on the evening of the Old Scholars' party. The time was fixed, and all that, and I went along to the telephone-box, as we'd arranged. I waited for the call. It did not come. I had to get home, and I was not really committed ... I did not feel I was committed ... to remain beyond the appointed time. So I left the telephone-box and went home.'

'And you really felt you were fulfilling your obligations?'

'Of course not,' replied the wretched man. 'But how could I have stayed out any longer?'

'You would know that better than I. Tell me, Mr Trench, what sort of message did you expect to get from Miss Faintley that evening?'

'I didn't know what to expect. My salary does not go far, and when Miss Faintley suggested that she was prepared to spend five pounds if I would accept a message, well, it was fixed up between us. I stood in the call-box quite a long time, but she didn't ring, and so, as it was rather a

nasty night, I went home, as I've told you, and thought no
more about it. I just concluded she had changed her mind,
and that I'd got very wet for nothing.'

'Almost as soon as you left the box, that call came
through. It was answered by an impartial witness who had
gone to the public call-box on his own account, and accidentally received Miss Faintley's message. When he heard
of her death he went to the police.'

'My God, then, I'm glad I wasn't there to take it myself!'

'Why do you say that?'

'It wouldn't do for the police to know I'd telephoned
Faintley. They always suspect the worst! I've never been
in any kind of trouble.'

'Didn't you think it odd that a fellow-member of your
school staff should offer you five pounds for answering a
telephone call?'

'She said it was a matter of life and death. I took it that
some near relative was ill.'

'And during a matter of life and death, Miss Faintley was
at a school party! It won't do, Mr Trench. You are not
doing yourself justice. You are an intelligent man ... a
professional man. Do you seriously tell me that that is what
you thought?'

'I didn't trouble to think at all. I needed the money
badly, and I was terribly disappointed not to get it. After
all, it was no business of mine to worry about what Faintley
was up to. I didn't give a damn! And I'm not answering
any more of these questions without a lawyer! Excuse me.
I have to get back to my boys.'

'One moment, Mr Trench,' said Mrs Bradley; and so
formidable was the strength of her personality and so persuasive her beautiful voice that the harassed man halted
half-way to the door and turned round. 'I am not a police
officer. I am a psychiatrist and a doctor. Why have you
allowed your wife to arrive at her present deplorable state?
Why don't you take her away from Kindleford to some
larger, more interesting place? She's killing herself. You
must know that. She has no friends, no interests, here, and

that is why she drinks as she does. You don't even take her on holiday.'

She half-expected a vituperative outburst from Trench. He did open his mouth and he flushed angrily. But then he regained control of himself, stared at the carpet, and said, with difficulty:

'She's ruined my life. Why should I do anything for her?'

'I don't need to answer that question. Look here, man, you cannot allow her to commit slow suicide. If you do, you are as much of a murderer as the man who killed Miss Faintley. Get her away! Show her some affection instead of the pious horror which you affect! Take her out of herself! If she wants to drink, have people in, and all get drunk together!'

Trench looked up. He had had enough of it.

'She's hopeless,' he said. 'You've seen her, of course, and you know. You're a — snooper! Keep your — nose out of my affairs, or I'll ...'

'Yes?' said Mrs Bradley calmly. She measured him with a mild, professional eye. 'How many times did you work with Miss Faintley? How convenient has it been to have a wife who was seldom in a condition to ask any questions? What were you doing on all those occasions when you did not attend school functions on the excuse of having an invalid at home?'

There was no doubt about the effect of *these* questions on Trench. All the hysterical bluster had disappeared. He looked older. His weak chin was shaking with horror. His eyes, as they caught hers, were begging for mercy.

'I swear,' he stammered, 'I swear I had nothing to do with Faintley's death. I swear it by ...'

'No, don't trouble,' said Mrs Bradley briskly. 'What you had better do is to go straight to the police as soon as school is over, and tell them everything you know. One thing in particular you *must* tell them. You must tell them that you are the person who met Miss Faintley in the cathedral city of Torbury, and you must explain to them the reason for your visit. I do not say confess to the murder. That might, at this stage, be going a little too far. By the way, I have a little present for you.' She took out an envelope and produced a small piece of fern. Trench gave a horrified moan.

She gave the sagging man a kindly pat on the arm and watched him stumble out of the room. The chisel he flung, as he turned round suddenly at the door, stuck in the wooden window-frame before it fell to the floor. Mrs Bradley darted to the door, slammed it shut behind him, shot the bolt which protected Miss Golightly from unauthorized visitors (especially from members of the staff who brought recalcitrant children to her or complaints against one another) and rang up the police.

CHAPTER TWELVE

CROMLECH DOWN BAY

*

'Look like the innocent flower,
But be the serpent under't.'

SHAKESPEARE – *Macbeth*

'But how could you possibly know?' demanded Laura, when, after Trench had been arrested for intent to cause bodily harm, Mrs Bradley was back at the Stone House.

'I did not know, child, but I interpreted a remark made by Mrs Trench.'

'You've told me what she said. I don't see anything to suggest that Trench was the person who caused Miss Faintley to "lose" Mark in Torbury, let alone that he murdered her at Cromlech.'

'Mrs Trench said that she had never had a holiday since the war, but she indicated that her husband had had a good many. She mentioned his excuse of attending the conferences organized by his professional association. I made a shot in the dark on the strength of this, and jockeyed Mr Trench into confirming that I had hit the target. Then, of course, he nearly hit *me*.'

'You know,' said Laura, shaking her head, 'you're the most immoral person I've met.'

'Murder is an immoral action, child.'

'All right. Where do we go from here?'

'Back to Cromlech to-morrow. Now that we know Miss Faintley's reason for taking Mark out and for being obliged to abandon him, we shall be able to check Mr Trench's account of his actions in Torbury, I hope. We have taken a

big step forward, and I am happy to compliment you upon
your efforts and to thank you for your co-operation.'

'Bow-wow-wow!' said Laura crudely. Mrs Bradley
cackled, but added seriously:

'As a matter of fact, I mean it. We should not have
arrived at this stage in the investigation unless you had
taken a post at the school and given us the benefit of your
knowledge of the staff.'

'Did Trench come across with anything valuable, then,
when you went with him to the police?'

'Valuable, and interesting too, although some of it was
lies, I fancy. He declared that he had had no outside-school
dealings with Miss Faintley until she asked him to answer
that telephone call. That I cannot believe because of what
follows. He went on to say that he left the telephone-box
not because he got tired of waiting, as the call was overdue
(which was what he told me in Miss Golightly's room at
school), but because a man had already rung him up in Miss
Faintley's name and had told him not to wait any longer, as
Miss Faintley was able, after all, to attend to the business
herself. Asked what the business was to be, he said he had
no idea. He was to be told over the telephone. Then he
went on to the subject of his visit to Torbury. He admitted
that he had met Miss Faintley there, but declared that the
meeting was accidental. He explained that Miss Faintley
thought it well to "lose" Mark because she was not anxious
to be the subject of a boy's gossip at school, for she supposed
that Mark would inevitably detail to his fellows that a man
and a woman teacher had met during the holidays, at a
town a considerable distance from their homes, and that
the boys would perceive something disingenuous in the
encounter.'

'Yes, they're all nasty-minded little brutes,' volunteered
Laura, with no note of criticism in her voice. 'Can't quite
see why you don't accept the innocent beginnings of his
evidence, though. I should have thought it would have been
safe enough to stick to it that he'd got tired of waiting in
the telephone-box, but highly dangerous to admit that he'd

met Faintley in Torbury, so near the scene of the murder, and only the day before it happened. Damn silly, too, to have chucked that chisel at you.'

'Yes, but don't you see, he doesn't realize that we possess no evidence (beyond his own confession) that he was ever in Torbury at that time.'

'It's a good thing you're not bound by Judges' Rules,' said Laura, grinning. 'But why don't you believe someone rang him up in Miss Faintley's name and put him off?'

'I neither believe nor disbelieve that. I am keeping an open mind. I am slightly inclined to disbelieve it because I am prejudiced by the fact that he changed his story, and I am slightly inclined to believe it because it does seem more likely that he was told not to wait any longer rather than that he –'

'Pushed off of his own accord, having got fed-up with hanging about on such a dirty night? Yes, with five pounds in the wind, I should think that *is* more likely,' agreed Laura. 'Oh, and I say!'

'Yes, I thought you'd remark upon that,' said Mrs Bradley, nodding like a bright-eyed mandarin but conveying no other impression of a Chinese, since she was wearing a dinner dress of mustard-coloured velvet, turquoise ear-rings, bracelets of Peruvian silver and a fob-watch. 'I should have been disappointed and disillusioned had that interesting and significant coincidence not occurred to you.'

'You mean the five pounds the shopkeeper gave Mandsell.'

'Exactly, child. It was always a fascinating thought that five whole pounds came so readily out of the till in a miserable little back-street draper's shop in a place like Kindleford, and on the afternoon after early-closing day.'

'I take it that Tomson thought Mandsell was really Trench. If he did, though, why did he behave high-hat with Mandsell?'

'Merely because he did not intend to give the receipt which Mandsell went back to demand.'

'But if he thought Mandsell was Trench, and knew that

Trench had been promised five pounds, why didn't he hand out the five pounds at once, in exchange for the parcel?'

'We asked him that when we confronted him with Trench this afternoon at the police station. He said he had forgotten the five pounds for the moment, and that the gentleman had seemed in a hurry. Then when the gentleman came back and began making a fuss, he remembered the five pounds which his "niece" had left with him, and handed them over, thinking to placate the gentleman, which, incidentally, they did.'

'What did he say when he saw Trench instead of Mandsell?'

'He behaved creditably. The man has the makings of a very pretty villain. He must have been considerably shaken when it dawned on him that he had reimbursed the wrong man, but, after staring at Trench in a way that made our schoolmaster look very uncomfortable, Tomson said that it *looked* like the same man, but he couldn't be sure. As you know, there's not the slightest resemblance except for a certain parity in height.'

'Cagey work! There's one thing, though. If Tomson didn't know he'd given the wrong man the money in the first place, it looks as if he didn't know Trench at all. Added to that, it is now obvious that the left-luggage clerk at Hagford didn't know Trench either. He'd been told to expect a man instead of Miss Faintley, and when Mandsell turned up he cheerfully gave him the parcel. On the other hand, when *I* went along to collect there was nothing doing. Very strange, as one would have thought he would have accepted me as an accredited agent, seeing that I came from the school.'

'Yes, but we already know, from that house on the cliffs at Cromlech and your own researches there, that we are investigating something bigger and more mysterious than a solitary murder. Miss Faintley was engaged in Kindleford upon work outside the scope of her school duties. She was not murdered for the sake of gain, nor was her murder a sex crime. She had no enemies of whom we know. Her death was brought about either because she had betrayed her trust, or because she had made some mistake which might prove dangerous to some other member of the gang. It seems to me likely, if not certain, that that member was Mr Trench.'

'Ha!' exclaimed Laura. 'Of course! I see it now. Woodwork! Trench made the flat case which Mandsell collected. But *why* did Trench leave that telephone-box before Faintley's call came through?'

'That is what we have to find out. It is possible that neither of Trench's explanations is the true one.'

'If Trench *did* make that wooden case, he's involved up to the neck, that's one thing, whether he did the actual murder or not. He's certainly got a murderer's mind. What did he think he'd gain, supposing the chisel *had* knocked you cold?'

'Reinstatement, I think. The gang must know that he killed Miss Faintley, and they must guess that she was killed because she was in possession of evidence that Trench had –'

'Let the issue down by walking out on the telephone call? Oh, yes, of course. But I still don't understand why Tomson didn't smell a rat when Mandsell walked in with that parcel. Faintley *couldn't* have described Trench so that it sounded like Mandsell. Tomson must have done a bit of swift thinking between Mandsell's first and second appearance in the shop, and decided that the wrong man had turned up.'

'But with the right parcel, child. Do not lose sight of that fact. It would, however, account, perhaps, for his refusing to give a receipt. It would give him a certain amount of bargaining power with his employers, the gang, if he could show (supposing that Mandsell turned awkward) that he had had his suspicions but had continued to carry out his orders. We had better ring up Inspector Darling the moment we've finished our coffee, and find out what he thinks of your suggestion.'

'He's bound to take it seriously,' said Laura, highly

pleased with herself. Before she could get to the telephone, however, it rang. She picked up the receiver and gave Mrs Bradley's exchange and number.

'Inspector Darling here,' said his voice. 'We've had a look round Trench's woodwork centre at the school. There doesn't seem much doubt of what he did in some of his spare time. Can I speak to Mrs Bradley herself, please?'

'Bother it. He's jumped my idea and got busy on it already!' said Laura, in disgust, as she handed over the receiver. Darling had certainly come to the conclusion that Trench's woodwork centre might repay investigation. He had taken with him what he hoped was a packing similar in size and thickness to the parcel which Mandsell had collected for Miss Faintley at Hagford Junction and which he had delivered to the rascally Tomson. Mandsell, only too anxious to co-operate with the police, had given, again to the best of his ability, the measurements of the parcel, but had anxiously pointed out that he was merely trusting to his memory. Tomson had remained unshakable in his two assertions that the parcel had been collected from him secretly, and that he had no idea of what it contained.

The inspector further reported the interview with Tomson.

'If you could smash up a statue, you could have opened a flat parcel,' Darling had pointed out. 'Didn't you *ever* have the urge, and open one?'

'No, I never opened one. They was sealed, and I didn't see how I could seal it up again with nobody being the wiser. And being as a plaster might get itself broke, well, a bit of wood wouldn't. Take my meaning?'

'Oh, the flat parcels *did* contain wood, then? You're sure of that?'

'How can I be sure when I tells you I never opened one? They *felt* like wood. That's all I can tell you. So what?'

With this information, for what it was worth, and Mandsell's evidence which corroborated it without adding to it, the Inspector had gone to the woodwork centre.

'Yes, Laura thought of that, too,' said Mrs Bradley.

'Good. We've found sufficient evidence here to hold Trench, apart from the incident of the chisel. What about Faintley now?'

'Trench is the murderer. Ask him how he disposed of the wooden cases when he had made them, and the date of the first one he made.'

'That's what I thought. Have you any plans of your own?'

'Yes. Laura and I return to Cromlech to-morrow.'

'I thought that is what you would say. Good luck to you, and keep Miss Menzies out of trouble.'

'The sparks fly upwards,' said Mrs Bradley non-committally. 'By the way, there may have been a fern in the parcel which Mr Mandsell collected from Hagford station – either *Asplenium Marinum* or *Polypodium Phegopteris*, I should say.'

'Come again, please?'

'Either the Sea Spleenwort or the Beech (read B.E.A.C.H.) Fern. That big case of ferns which two men, seen by Miss Menzies, removed from Cromlech House, went away by sea. But don't bother about that. Push Mr Trench as far as he will go. It won't help much, except negatively. You will find, I think, that he took the wooden cases to someone at Hagford station who sent them on to the plotters, who put the requisite variety of fern into them and sent them back to Hagford to be collected by Miss Faintley.'

'But why such an elaborate arrangement?'

'In order that the left hand should not know what the right hand was doing.'

'Quite a sound principle on secret service, ma'am. I've no doubt that's the right answer. We've quite lost the trail of that left-luggage clerk. He's vanished. We've not even found the other two men named Price who went for the tour. They are obviously members of the gang who aided the real Prices' getaway. We've pulled in the stammering clerk who refused to give Miss Menzies the parcel, but he seems as innocent as the day. We shall keep the tabs on him, of course, but I don't think much will come of it.'

Mrs Bradley travelled at the sedate pace decreed by George the chauffeur from Wandles Parva to Cromlech, and Laura went by sea and joined her employer at the hotel where they had stayed on their previous visit. The manager made them welcome.

'Funny,' said Laura. 'I thought they might hate the sight of us here, this time, what with Faintley getting herself murdered during our last visit, and the police dodging about, and all that.'

'It is a mistake to assume that notoriety of that sort is necessarily harmful to a hotel, and in any case we were not much involved except that you discovered the body. Where did you leave the cruiser?'

'The usual anchorage. There's not much stuff about to-day, so it should be very easy to get away from there to-morrow. I take it you mean to go round by sea, as I did, and take that zigzag road to the house. I hope you are going armed and well prepared. Now Trench is arrested and Tomson is being pushed so hard that he may crack at any moment, and two real Prices and two pseudo-Prices are being hunted by the gendarmes, I can imagine healthier occupations than yours!'

'I do not anticipate trouble up at that house. Adventure, I feel, will come later. And now, to bed, for we must be up betimes!' said Mrs Bradley.

But bed was farther off than she anticipated, for as they went from the lounge to the foot of the stairs they were waylaid.

'A telephone call for Mrs Lestrange Bradley!'

She took it whilst Laura waited. When she emerged her saurian smile was eloquent of excellent news. Laura asked no questions, and when they reached their first-floor landing Mrs Bradley drew her secretary into her room.

'A most helpful piece of information,' she announced. 'Mr Trench seems to have decided to confide in the police on condition that they keep him in close custody. It is obvious that he is far more afraid of what he can expect from the gang than of being found guilty of attempted murder ... a strangely disquieting comment on our so-called civilization, but one to which, thanks to the Dictators, we are becoming more and more accustomed.'

'What has he told the police?'

'That he has sent a consignment of six wooden packings to a place called Damp House, Bridbay, Isle of Wight. Well, well, Inspector Darling, I have no doubt, will keep the gyves on him for more reasons than one. Well, now, we start at six in the morning, for if we are to add a trip to the Isle of Wight to our schedule we shall have a long day.'

The manager, who, far from deprecating Mrs Bradley's activities, felt that they shed lustre upon his hotel, insisted upon giving them breakfast before they set out, and waited upon them himself. A discreet man, an ex-Regular officer, he asked no questions but wished them a pleasant trip.

By seven they were on board the *Canto Five* and were nosing out to give the great headland a wide berth in a choppy sea. It was not long before Laura was anchoring in the bay.

'Now what's the programme?' she inquired.

'I want you to put me ashore and then come back on board.'

'Thus missing any possibility of some fun! I call that hard.'

'Yes, but I have been thinking things over. We are almost as far off as ever from solving the mystery of Miss Faintley's death, although we assume that we know now who murdered her. We know she worked for people whose desire for secrecy is so keen that they have invented this fantastic code based on the names of British ferns in order to communicate with one another. Their actions are probably, but not undoubtedly, criminal, and Miss Faintley may or may not have been murdered at their instigation ... personally, I don't think she was, but let that pass.'

'But we know the house up there was their haunt, and that's where her body was found!'

'True; so you are justified in assuming that they *were* concerned in her death. Unfortunately, except for their (to us unimportant) satellites, Miss Faintley, Trench, and Tomson, we have not the slightest idea of the identity of any members of the gang, unless the police find Price and Mr Mandsell can swear to him.'

'I wish we could get hold of one of those ferns they pack in the flat parcels.'

'So do I, indeed. Those sent in the plaster statues appear to be warnings, but those packed in Mr Trench's wood blocks must be instructions or information of plans. I have toyed with the notion of sending a similar package to Hagford Junction to see what happened, but I doubt whether the results would be helpful.'

'Quite so. Let us make for the shore.'

Laura rowed her ashore, watched her until she rounded the first bend of the zigzag path to the house, and then moodily returned to the cruiser. She smoked a cigarette and then decided to bathe. It was while she was in the water, fairly close inshore, that the dredger turned up. For some time Laura was unaware of its approach, for it was hidden from her by the hull of her own boat, and, by the time she spotted it, it was drawing towards an anchorage in the east-ward arm of the bay. It anchored, and set to work, an uninspiring bucket-dredger of ancient pattern, setting its chain of buckets to dredge up sand from the sea-bed. Laura, wiping salt water from her face with a wet wrist, gazed interestedly, for there seemed no purpose in dredging at such a spot. There was no river-mouth and no harbour. The apparently pointless work went on for more than two hours, during which time she got dry and dressed. She ate some chocolate, sunbathed on the cabin roof in suntop and linen shorts, ate an apple, smoked another cigarette, went down to the tiny galley and made some tea, and speculated all the time on the chances of Mrs Bradley's having walked into trouble up at the mysterious house.

There were a fair number of people on the beach by this time, and a couple of boys, on floats, came out to have a look at her boat. Laura was glad of company and conversed amiably with them as they paddled slowly round the cruiser.

She asked them whether the dredger was often there, and if they knew why the bay needed deepening. One of them volunteered the information that she was dredging on the site of a supposed wreck which had had bullion on board. He had gathered this from talk at the hotel where he was staying. One of the local boatmen, it was understood, had gone out to the dredger to pass the time of day and ask whether they wanted to buy shellfish. He had never heard of any wreck, but thought it must date from the war and had been hushed up for some reason.

'I thought they generally used divers to get stuff up from wrecks,' said Laura. 'I don't see what you could expect to get up in those buckets, unless it might be proof that you'd found the right spot. And they haven't got a hopper alongside, and nothing is dumped in the hold. All that sand and stuff just keeps getting put back again. It all seems such a waste of time.'

The boys paddled shorewards, and Laura went below to scrape potatoes. She had no idea of when she might expect Mrs Bradley, but there seemed no harm in getting lunch ready to cook. When she came on deck again the dredger was entertaining a visitor. A rusty-looking sea-going cruiser had joined her and was taking on board some wooden crates. After a bit, with a farewell toot of her siren, she was off, bumping choppily but going fast, and was soon out of sight round the headland. The dredger had ceased work some time previously, and now sheered off, out to sea. Laura watched until she disappeared over the horizon. When the girl looked shorewards again, somebody was signalling from the beach. Laura turned the binoculars on to the small figure and was relieved to discover that it was, as she had hoped, Mrs Bradley.

'Still in one piece,' thought Laura. 'Thank goodness for that! Wonder whether she's found out anything useful?'

She cast off in the dinghy and rowed to the beach.

'The house has been used again,' said Mrs Bradley, when they were once more on board *Canto Five*. 'An unwithered frond of *Asplenium Septentrionale,* the Forked Spleenwort, was lying just inside the front door. I climbed in by means of the back window, which, since the police broke it, has not been mended.'

'Anything else interesting?'

'No, not to me. Apart from *Asplenium Septentrionale,* there was nothing to discover except the cellar.'

'I don't remember seeing a cellar door.'

'No. It is a trap-door, covered by matting, in the floor of that one furnished room.'

'I wonder why they didn't shove Faintley's body into the cellar? Nobody would ever have found it.'

'The cellar is not very large and a body might have been in the way. Besides, bodies *do* decompose, you know.'

'Did you expect to find a cellar?'

'No, but I always look under rugs and mats and the like as a matter of course because of my interest in priest's holes and church crypts.'

'Anything interesting on the cliff-top?'

'I regret to emphasize that there was nothing interesting at all. Nevertheless, I was inclined to be sorry I had not taken you along. You would have enjoyed it. It was gloriously hot on the headland, and the scent of the gorse was very pleasing.'

'It's been a bit boring here except for the dredger that dredged up sand, and the story of a wreck that doesn't seem to have happened.' She described her morning while the potatoes were boiling. Mrs Bradley was interested in the story of the dredger. 'I wonder whether you'd mind if I shifted over after lunch and dropped anchor just about where *they* did?' Laura concluded. 'There must have been some method in the madness, but I'm hanged if I can spot what it was. You don't think there was any connexion between the dredger and the people we're after, do you? It wasn't doing its proper job, and it *did* unload those packing-cases on to the cruiser.'

'I was wondering, child. If there were some reason for hanging about, to pretend to be dredging would be as good a way as any of appearing to have legitimate business, I should think. Move over, by all means. I doubt whether we shall learn anything, but one never knows. You cannot tell, of course, whether the cabin cruiser was the one which may have shipped away the case of ferns?'

The move, made as soon as the washing-up was done, gave them no help. Mrs Bradley, while Laura lazed and digested her lunch before dropping overboard for a swim, studied the cliff-face earnestly through binoculars, but there was nothing to be seen but the gulls.

Laura's deep dives, when she had gone in for her dip, were equally unproductive. After tea she took up anchor and slid away on a longish north-east slant to attempt to get some satisfactory evidence from the clue supplied by Mr Trench's confession to the police. The sun began to dip, the sea grew calm as the breeze died, and Laura, who had studied the *Yachtsman's Pilot* until she could have drawn in her sleep the plan of the harbour entrance she wanted, took the wheel from Mrs Bradley as the Isle of Wight loomed larger, and made for the western end of the island.

Mrs Bradley, standing beside her with the binoculars trained on the land, said suddenly:

'There's your dredger, child, in that little bay ahead of us. Put your helm over. We don't want to get near enough for the men on board to recognize this as the cruiser which shared the bay with them this morning. It won't matter if they are on their lawful occasions, but, if they are not, we don't want to give the impression that we are following them about. I also find that rusty cruiser interesting. I wish I knew whether it took off those two men and the large case of ferns – and, if it did, whether the people on board her recognized *Canto Five* when they saw her again.'

'They seemed too busy loading those stores – whatever they were – to notice anything, but you never know. Anyway, even if they *did* recognize her, there's no reason why they should connect her with anything to their disadvantage, is there?'

'No, but if their occasions are unlawful they are bound

to be deeply suspicious. I am very anxious not to arouse their suspicions, because, if we do –'

'They'll merely lead us a dance, and we shan't be any nearer to a solution of our problem. Yes, I see what you mean. All right, we'll steer clear for a bit. As the dredger is anchored off the Isle of Wight, perhaps the cruiser will turn up there, too.'

CHAPTER THIRTEEN

OPERATION DREDGER

*

'. . . but the entrance demands only ordinary caution.'
E. KEBLE CHATTERTON – *The Yachtsman's Pilot*

'WHERE are we making for, child?' asked Mrs Bradley, later.

'Well, I'm not going to put in to Lymington if I can help it,' said Laura, 'with those British Railway steamers bucketing past and the stream of the Solent acting horrid, as it's bound to do after a day like this, I should think. What about making for the Beaulieu River, and then creeping back on the trail?'

'It is your cruiser,' said Mrs Bradley, 'and I should think that would do very nicely, except that we mustn't let them get away from us, and we don't want to meet any liners coming out from Southampton.'

'They're mostly away by five on this tide, I think, and probably the railway steamers have finished for the day. What about Keyhaven? By the time we're behind Hurst Castle they won't be able to pick us out, and it will look as though we're going to find moorings there for the night. Then, when we like, we can cross towards the Isle of Wight and pick up the trail again from there. We'll have to moor until dusk, and then we're not likely to be recognized if we have to go fairly close to them.'

Keyhaven was small, and a number of yachts and cruisers had permanent moorings there. The tide was sufficient, and Laura knew enough to keep clear of eddies. She picked up the leading marks, and went in.

The mud-flats on either side of the anchorage were

covered with marshy grass and, except for Hurst Fort, to the south-east, there was no eminence on the low-lying shores. They remained stationary long enough for Laura to row the dinghy to the steps near the inn, where she purchased a quart of beer and made inquiries about moorings.

By the time she got back to *Canto Five* it was becoming dark, so she suggested to Mrs Bradley that they might as well have a quick meal and then move off. They put on their lights and chugged steadily and slowly past a single line of moored craft until they gained the entrance and were off Old Pier but some distance from it. The High Light was already functioning, and they soon left it almost directly behind them as they crossed the narrowest part of the Solent and made for the shore of the Isle of Wight near Sconce Point. Here Laura steered north-east, and crawled round the coast to the little bay for which the dredger had made. It was still just sufficiently light for them to recognize her unmistakable silhouette with the erection to take the bucket-chain, and the buckets themselves slanting stiffly from amidships towards and under the crane in her bows. She was squat, utilitarian and ugly, almost a repulsive sight except for her funnel, which had the comical effect of having been borrowed from the *Rocket* and stuck on like a clown's hat in a pantomime.

'Something frightfully squamous about dredgers,' muttered Laura. 'Where do we go from here?'

'Anchor at the farther end of the bay. Then we'll row off in the dinghy, beach her, and stroll along the shore to see what can be seen. The moon is up, so the darker it gets now the better. We should be able to find some vantage-point from which we can observe without ourselves being noticed.'

This proved easy enough. The beach was sandy on an outgoing tide, and behind it rose cliffs which offered shadowed nooks in any one of which it was possible to hide. They strolled by the edge of the water for a time, and, as they approached the anchorage of the dredger, they altered course to gain the shadow of the cliffs. In the first alcove they tried, Laura almost fell over a courting couple, but except for these, and three girls who were taking a stroll by the edge of the water, there seemed to be nobody about. They found a suitable spot and sat down on the rubble which at some time had fallen from the cliff.

The dredger was correctly lighted, but not a sound came from her, although they sat there for over an hour.

'I'm going to paddle the dinghy out to her and have a look-see,' said Laura. 'I don't believe there's anybody on board.'

'Then I'm coming, too, dear child.'

They returned to the dinghy, now exposed by the moonlight, pushed off, and stepped aboard, wet, but (in Laura's case), happy to be doing something active. It did not take long to reach the dredger, for the tide did most of the work. They reached her to find a rope-ladder trailing over the side.

They shipped their oars and Laura caught hold of the anchor-chain and pulled the dinghy close in to the side of the dredger. The manoeuvres, although they had been carried out with caution, had not been soundless, so, whilst the dinghy gently eased herself up and down, Laura and her employer listened intently. There was nothing to be heard, however, except the lazy slap of the outgoing tide against the shoreward side of the dredger, so, after a while, Laura muttered:

'Unship your right-hand oar, and, when I say *Now*, pull us round a bit so that we're stern-on to this anchor-chain. I'm going aboard.'

Mrs Bradley felt for the small revolver which she had carried all day in her skirt-pocket. She was almost certain that there was nobody on board, but she did not intend to take chances.

'Right,' she said. Laura shifted her grip on the anchor-chain.

'*Now!*' she said, and as the dinghy came round she stood up and made a cat-jump. The anchor-chain slackened suddenly, and Laura, afraid of smashing herself against the hull, let go and fell into the sea. She came up, spitting, and swam round to where they had seen the rope-ladder dangling over the side. Up this she went hand over hand, and climbed aboard. Mrs Bradley, who had heard the splash and guessed not only what had happened but what Laura would do, appeared on the seaward side of the dredger again and caught Laura's softly-muttered 'O.K. I'm aboard'.

It was soon certain that she was alone on the ship. She had never been on a dredger before and at any other time would have been interested in its machinery and gear; but, for one thing, below deck everything was dark, and, for another, there might be no time to lose. By the time she had groped her way down a slippery iron companion-ladder to the cabin she had made so much noise that she must, she thought, have awakened even the heaviest sleeper, if he were on board. She was about to feel her way on deck again . . . for it was uncomfortably eerie on the dredger . . . when she bit her tongue in nervous astonishment as a voice in the darkness said:

'*Polypodium Vulgare,* dammit! *Polypodium Vulgare,* dammit! *Polypodium Vulgare,* curse your silly eyes!'

'Good Lord!' said Laura, recovering her nerve. 'Captain Flint in person! All right, Polly! Pretty Polly, then!'

'*Lastrea Filix-Mas! Lastrea Filix-Mas! Filix-Mas! Filix-Mas! Filix-Mas!*' screamed the parrot. Laura wasted no more time on blandishments. She crawled up on deck and called over the side to the occupant of the dinghy:

'Nobody here but a parrot saying . . . get it, quick, while I remember . . . *Polypodium Vulgare, dammit* and *Lastrea Filix-Mas.* Doesn't mean a thing to me, unless it's some more of those ferns. Shall I risk putting on a light in the cabin, do you think?'

'No. Come half-way down the rope-ladder and I'll give you my torch. Are your hands dry?'

'Yes. I've rubbed them dry groping about up here. Wasn't I an ass to fall in? I'm squelching water all over the place!'

The torch changed hands at the third attempt, and Laura, taking the ends of the large handkerchief (in which

Mrs Bradley had cradled and tied the small torch) between her teeth, climbed aboard again.

With the torch to aid her, a search of the interior of the dredger was simple but unrewarding. The parrot had turned either sulky or sleepy, and did not utter again except to give an indignant squeal as the tiny beam of light invaded its cage. Except for an empty wine-bottle and the remains of a loaf of bread on a wooden platter with a knife beside it on the cabin table, there was no indication (but for the presence of the parrot) that any human being had set foot on board until Laura's own arrival, and she was about to return to the deck and so to the dinghy when she said aloud:

'Crass idiot! *Think*, woman, *think!*'

Having thus addressed herself, she put Mrs Bradley's torch with some difficulty into the sopping-wet pocket of her slacks, picked up the knife by the tip of the blade and, folding the bottle-neck in Mrs Bradley's handkerchief, she essayed the companion-way once more. Risking every moment being precipitated backwards by the motion of the anchored vessel, which, although not heavy, was more than a little noticeable to a person with both hands full, Laura managed to get up on deck.

'I say!' she called over the side. 'I've impounded two fingerprinted objects. Do you suppose they're any good?'

'The police, no doubt, will think so, but if you bring them away with you the persons who have charge of this vessel will know that someone has been on board. I think we might risk that, though.'

'They'd know, anyway. I've dripped everywhere. I've got a wine-bottle and a bread-knife. Only thing is, I don't know how to get them down to the dinghy. If only it was an iron ladder instead of rope! How can we manage? I can bring the knife down between my teeth, I suppose, but I don't know what to do about the bottle.'

'Is it empty?'

'Yes, and it's got the cork in it.'

'Drop it overboard into a patch of moonlight and I'll retrieve it if I can. The sea won't wash off fingerprints if they are reasonably oily, and, fortunately, most of them are!'

With their treasure trove, as Laura deprecatingly and jokingly called it, they returned straightway to the cruiser, and Laura changed her clothes.

'And now for old Trench's tip, and the Damp House . . . funny name! . . . at Bridbay,' said Laura, starting up her engine. 'Hope we don't run into our returning sand-dredgers going round the next point!'

They ran into nothing except the moonlight, and in less than half an hour were between the leading-beacons at the entrance to Bridbay Harbour. As they passed the beacons and were rounding the bend between the lighted buoys which showed the way to the anchorage, the clock on a nearby church struck the witching hour.

'Midnight, and all well,' murmured Laura, as the anchor went in. 'Now where's the dump we're after, I wonder?'

'We must wait for dawn,' said Mrs Bradley. 'For one thing, we'd better have some sleep, and, for another, we can't go looking for the house at this time of night.'

'I'm hungry, too,' said Laura. 'We've had nothing except that biscuit and cheese and beer at Keyhaven since we had our lunch.'

'Quite so. You will turn in while I get some soup and sandwiches ready.'

'Don't trouble about sandwiches for me! A thick slice or two of tinned tongue and a couple of wedges of bread and butter will do me fine. You haven't told me yet what you make of the parrot's Latin or whatever it was.'

'I am extremely interested in the parrot's conversation, and extremely grateful to the parrot,' Mrs Bradley responded. '*Polypodium Vulgare* is the Common Polypody, and stands, possibly, in the fern code, for Our Men, or something of that sort. I deduced this from the parrot's habit of following up the repetition of the name with the irritable "dammit". This indicates, of course, that some stupid or uneducated person was being given a password which would reveal that he was a member of the gang to other members. The parrot's second repetition, *Lastrea Filix-Mas*, the Male Fern, is, just possibly, the code name by which the leader of the gang is known. There is a certain arrogance about the choice of this name which causes me to think it may be –'

'The boss's signature-tune? Sounds all right. Of course, we've nothing to go on.'

'Except *Asplenium Septentrionale*, the Forked Spleenwort, indicating, I think, that two attempts at something are to be made. But I admit this is all so much guesswork, and my reading of the fern-code is possibly ludicrously wrong. Here is your soup, and I have added baked beans from a tin.'

Just as the cruiser's portholes began to turn grey, Laura, who throve and flourished on an average of three hours sleep a night, rose from her bunk and went on deck. The harbour water was a sea of mist and near the *Canto Five* lay yachts and cruisers of all sizes and many designs, but she could not see far enough to know whether the rusty cruiser which had taken stores from the dredger was in the harbour or not.

'Go and look for our friends if you want to, while I get breakfast,' said Mrs Bradley's voice behind her. 'A towel and a bathing cap are sufficient camouflage, I think.'

Laura went below, exchanged her pyjamas for a bikini, draped the largest towel she could find around her powerful and beautiful shoulders, pulled on her swimming cap and dropped into the dinghy.

The morning brightened rapidly and the baffling haze on the water began to lift. She spotted the rusty cruiser with a thrill of joy, and marked its position. It was lying almost under the drawbridge, close to the steps, a fact which seemed to indicate that its crew had business ashore.

Laura sculled on, under the bridge, which carried a toll-road inland. Beyond the buoyed channel and the toll-house, she found a suitable spot to swim. The water was cold at that time in the morning, and breakfast, she thought, must not be long delayed, so she contented herself with a brisk five minutes in the water, and then, draping the towel around her almost naked body, she rowed rapidly back to *Canto Five.*

There was grape-fruit, cereal, toast and scrambled eggs for breakfast, and the crew did not stop to wash up, but, while the morning was still very young, they went ashore and tied up at the steps near which the rusty cruiser was moored.

No one was visible or audible on board her, and Laura would have been tempted to try the tactics which she had already carried out on the dredger, but time pressed if they were to find Damp House before the village was stirring.

They crossed the drawbridge, placed the fee on the toll-house window-sill – the gates had been left open – and came into the village past the harbour-master's house and the post office. At the end of the next street was a fourteenth-century church, and not far away were some shops and a small hotel. Beyond the hotel was a long, narrow pier and nothing else, but between the back of the post office and the land-ward side of the hotel was a narrow lane of concrete which led back to the harbour. To the right, another lane led to the castle, refortified during the war to control the entrance as it had done in the Middle Ages. Between the castle and the harbour wall was a house of moderate size with heavily-curtained windows and a door which had neither letter-box, knocker, name nor number.

'This might be it,' said Laura, 'but we'd better finish exploring, I suppose. If it *is* it, I wonder what Trench meant by calling it Damp House?'

They finished exploring the village, and even walked a mile or so up the hill which bore the only inland road, but no dwelling was named Damp House.

'Well, the first thing to do when the post office opens is to telephone Detective-Inspector Vardon and tell him where *we* are and where the highly-suspect dredger is. Then he can make up his mind what to do,' said Mrs Bradley. 'I shall also tell him about the parrot with the remarkable turn of speech. There is no doubt that we are on the right track. After we have sent out our message, the next thing to do will be to keep a watch on this house, and how that is to be managed without ourselves being detected, I confess that at the moment I do not know.'

'Let's get back to the cruiser and plan the campaign. Then, when we come ashore again, you can send your message to the cops and I'll go and interview the harbour-master.'

'An excellent idea,' said Mrs Bradley. As they walked back to the steps beside which the dinghy was moored, Laura suddenly said:

'Come to think of it, what did you make of Miss Franks' admission that Faintley had asked her for a loan of four hundred pounds?'

'Interesting and possibly instructive. I have thought about that a good deal. Miss Faintley had her salary which, although in one sense inadequate, was enough to live on; she rented, but had not bought, the flat for herself and her aunt, yet she asked for the loan, and must have needed it pretty badly if she thought that Miss Franks would supply it, for Miss Franks, no doubt, has the Jewish sense of money values. I think that at some time we might contact Miss Franks again. That four hundred pounds might be significant.'

'And, meanwhile, what do we do?'

'Thereby, as they say, hangs a tale. Pray step into your dinghy and let us go.'

Laura complied with this polite request, and they were soon back on board *Canto Five*.

'What did you mean by saying thereby hangs a tale?' Laura inquired, as she sat on the cabin-top and stared out to sea.

'How soon can you see the harbour-master?' Mrs Bradley inquired.

'Any time after nine, I expect. Why?'

'His house might afford an excellent base from which to keep an eye on our suspects, if the nameless house near his is the one we want.'

'Yes, I'd thought of that. But how do we get him to play ball?'

'I will telephone first. The rest should then be easy.'

'Sez you, with all respect. But we can try.'

As soon as the church clock struck nine, Mrs Bradley went ashore in the dinghy while Laura washed up the breakfast dishes. Mrs Bradley was back inside half an hour.

'Give the Inspector time to telephone the harbour-master,' she said, 'and then I think you can go ahead.'

The harbour-master was an old sailor. He was friendly and obliging, and would have been so, Laura concluded, even without the knowledge that their errand was of public importance. As it was, he had agreed to allow her to use a window on the first floor of his house if the police report justified this, so that she could keep a watch on the house without a name. What part Mrs Bradley proposed to play while she herself was thus employed, Laura did not know, and she was too well-disciplined to inquire about it. She was startled, however, by Mrs Bradley's next question.

'You remember Alice Boorman, who was a member of your particular trio at College, dear child?'

'Very definitely. We still correspond. I met her the year before last in Paris, if you recollect, where she was in charge of some gawping lassies from the top class of her school. She was always an earnest old cuckoo.'

'Am I right in believing that she was in the Advanced Biology group?'

'You certainly are. What young Alice doesn't know about cutting sections and sticking them under the microscope is not knowledge. Why, if I may be permitted to ask, does her name crop up in the present nostalgic and moving conversation?'

'If it had not, the conversation would be neither nostalgic nor moving. Do not revert to the style of your mis-spent youth. Give me Miss Boorman's address.'

'Littledene, Bosworth Road, Graftonbury-under-the-Edge. Why? . . . and, equally, why a bloke with her talents wants to bury herself alive in a place like that is more than I can fathom. But, there! I never did understand the dear old scout, and that's a fact.'

'Mutual lack of understanding is not necessarily detrimental to mutual abiding friendship. Thank you. I shall send Miss Boorman a telegram to find out how much she knows about British ferns.'

'*Oh!*' said Laura, who had been squinting down her nose in disapproval of all Mrs Bradley's remarks except the last one. 'Oh, I *see!* Now why didn't *I* think of that?'

'Because you had not thought of laying a false trail for our friends. I will go ashore again and send my telegram, and by the time I get back it will be all right, I should think, for you to go to the harbour-master again. Of course, if the police have been non-co-operative, please do not attempt to watch the house from any other vantage-point. I do not desire to waste my time attending an inquest. In the harbour-master's house you will be perfectly safe, but if these people are what I suspect them to be –'

'What *do* you suspect them to be? I've been rummaging in my head for three weeks now, and I can't make a selection from my ideas. I've thought of every kind of illegality from various smuggled articles to Communist infiltration, gun-running, forged banknotes and piracy. They all seem equally possible. It must be something pretty steep if Trench was prepared to murder Faintley to keep their secrets.'

'Or to keep secret the fact that he had failed to keep his appointment with her. Remember, we still do not know why he failed.'

'Everything about that telephone business is dashed peculiar, you know.'

'Indeed, yes. What prompted her to arrange that he should go to Hagford and collect that particular parcel we shall never know except by a stroke of good fortune, but it was probably some perfectly simple reason such as that she had already booked her holiday accommodation at Cromlech and did not see why she should postpone her vacation in order to get a parcel which could equally well be picked up and taken to Tomson's shop by somebody else.'

'Yes, I see. And she couldn't ask anybody else because they would have wondered what the devil she was up to, having dealings with a scruff like Tomson. So it had to be Trench, who was partly in the swim, or else nobody.'

'Exactly. Then what I think happened was this: Miss Faintley was very well paid for what she did, and it troubled her conscience (it is amazing to the amoral minds of our generation ... or it would be if they ever used their brains for anything but their own personal advantage ... to find how extremely, almost morbidly, conscientious are teachers and Civil Servants) that she had relegated a task for which she had agreed to take responsibility to someone who might or might not have carried out her instructions.'

'So she sent Trench a telegram to ask whether all was well, and he sent back to say he'd left the phone-box before her message came through. So, feeling thoroughly windy, she sent for him and arranged to meet him in Torbury, taking young Mark with her as camouflage and bent on losing him immediately. Yes, I can see all that. What I *can't* see is why she didn't instruct Trench by word of mouth. Why all this risky and uncertain business of the public call-box method?'

'Just that she found no opportunity of speaking to him privately at school. She could have sent him a note by one of the children to ask him whether he would agree to be in the call-box at a particular time as she had a message for him, and he could write back to agree. She would not commit herself further on paper, no doubt, as secrecy had been urged upon her from the beginning. You probably know better than I do how very difficult it can be ... particularly on a mixed staff in a school ... to obtain an opportunity for a really private conversation.'

'By Jove, yes, you're right there. So the sweet Alice is to collect and transmit ferns, is she? No doubt she has sources from which she can obtain plants and things for her school work. Even *I* was told where to send to for my nature stuff, and told to be *very* economical!'

'At any rate, we can see. The time-lag between the sending of my telegram and the receipt of her parcels may make a difficulty, but we must hope for the best. Thanks to the talking parrot, we know that we are on the right track, and now that the rusty-looking cruiser is in harbour with us, I feel that we may soon expect developments. I only hope we have selected the right house!'

'There's one more point: why did she need Mark for camouflage? She could have gone trotting off by herself, arriving with guide book and plan of city showing position of cathedral, etc., couldn't she?'

'My theory there is that she recognized one of the gang in Cromlech. It was surely not quite coincidental that she chose for her holiday the resort where the gang had one of their headquarters ... the house on the cliff ... but she may have had a shock at recognizing in the village someone whom she had not expected to see there. She probably thought that he had been following and spying on her because of her failure to collect the parcel, and she summoned Trench, in a fit of panic, to meet her and report that the parcel had indeed been delivered to Tomson ... an assurance which Trench was quite unable to give. It was because he was unable to give it that he murdered her, I think ... another example of panic. She took Mark to avoid being followed by the person she had recognized –'

'This is where we want some dates, you know.'

'We have them. I copied them from the visitors' book at the hotel. Miss Faintley had been in Cromlech six days before she was murdered, counting the day she came down.'

'So the man she recognized –!'

'Exactly. The man she recognized could have been the left-luggage clerk at Hagford ... the missing Price. Had it been anyone else I don't think she would have worried. No doubt she had been summoned to Cromlech for some instructions which could not be confided in writing or over the telephone, and which the fern-code could not sufficiently clearly express. But when she saw Price, her conscience made a coward of her, and Trench's fears made a murderer out of him.'

CHAPTER FOURTEEN

DAMP HOUSE

*

'Let what there needs be done. Stay! with him one companion,
His deacon, Dirvan: Warm twice over must the welcome be,
But both will share one cell.'

GERARD MANLEY HOPKINS – *St Winefred's Well*

'So that's the argument,' said Laura thoughtfully. 'Faintley
had been summoned for a conference and recognized Price,
who ought to have been at Hagford railway station. Still,
he was on holiday. Something he said must have given her
the clue, I suppose, that things had gone wrong about the
parcel, so she sent for Trench. Trench realized that he was
in a spot if she reported him to the bosses, so he met her at
Torbury station and suggested they go to Cromlech Down
House for a show-down, and there he murdered her. Maybe
he had been instructed to murder her. Oh, well, it's all
speculation, so far, but it may be as far as we'll get.'

Mrs Bradley did not share this pessimistic view. The
harbour-master, contacted on the telephone by the police,
came off to *Canto Five* in his launch and invited Laura to
make what use she liked of his house. There was an upstair
window from which she could watch the Damp House. He
had never heard it called that, he observed. It had been
used as a clubhouse by people calling themselves the
Burgee Mariners, but that was before the war. It belonged
now to a man named Shagg, who used it at week-ends
and in holiday times, and often had friends to stay with
him.

'That's his boat, that rusty contraption out there,' the
harbour-master added. 'She's got a Thames registration, so

I suppose that's where he keeps her when she's not down here.'

This information clinched the matter. The Damp House was identified. Laura settled down in a first-floor room to keep watch. Lunch was brought to her at one o'clock, and long before tea-time she was feeling extremely bored. There were very few people about and those that there were did not come into her view for more than a moment, but made for the shops, the post office or the hotel. After three in the afternoon there descended a kind of doldrums on the harbour channel also, and as the house she was watching seemed as empty as a robbed and rifled grave, Laura heartily wished herself back on *Canto Five*. Tea, brought at half past four, was an extremely welcome diversion, so much so that, although she dutifully kept her eyes on the window, Laura almost missed seeing the rusty cruiser putting out to sea. To her astonishment, *Canto Five* did not follow.

'Wonder what Mrs Croc. has got up her sleeve?' thought Laura. 'I should have been after them like a shot. Wonder whether they came from shore, or whether they were already there and popped up from the cabin?'

Her speculations were cut short by the arrival of a small sailing boat of the Tumlare class, double-ended and fast, with only one man aboard her. That he knew his job was evident, and Laura, with one eye on Damp House, watched him come up to moorings with the appreciation of one expert for the work of another.

When he rowed ashore in his tiny dinghy, she saw, to her astonishment, that it was Bannister. Very shortly afterwards there was a knock at the door, and the harbour-master's wife came up to say that Mrs Bradley and a gentleman would be glad of a word and that she would show them up.

'But what are *you* doing down here? You ought to be at school!' exclaimed Laura, when her erstwhile colleague and her employer came into the room.

'I'm on sick leave,' said Bannister, grinning, 'medical certificate and all, so I thought I'd come along and see what you were up to.'

Laura glanced at her employer.

'You sent for him,' she said. 'That means a rough-house. Anything for a change. I'm bored to tears. By the way, why did you let *Rusty* get away from us? I could hardly believe my eyes when I saw her going over towards Lymington.'

'She won't go to Lymington, child. She will alter course and make for the dredger. The birds are attempting to fly, but they will not get far. Detective-Inspector Vardon and the local police force already, if my message has not miscarried, are in possession of the dredger, and the Customs and Excise officials will, no doubt, take charge of the cabin cruiser.'

'But it may not be a case for the Customs.'

'If it is not, no harm will have been done. There are only two men on board. They came on a motor cycle combination over the toll-bridge. I do not think they will give the officers much trouble.'

'So we miss the last of the fun, and we still don't know what their game is, or what the ferns mean, or whether Trench really murdered Faintley!'

'Be of good cheer. Mr Bannister has offered to remain here with you until nightfall, and as soon as it is dark you may return to *Canto Five* and he will go back on board his yacht.'

Laura, who was feeling disgruntled, disclaimed any need for companionship, so Mrs Bradley grinning like an alligator and Bannister looking disappointed, the two left the harbour-master's house and Laura was left again in solitude.

The harbour-master produced a battery-operated radio set for her amusement, but the long summer evening passed slowly, and still nothing happened. Dusk fell at last, and Laura, thankful to the darkness and to her hosts, slipped out and was about to cross between the hotel and the post office when a light was put on in the house she had been watching. Laura took cover and was rewarded for her long hours of fruitless vigil when the front door opened and a man stood there silhouetted against the light. She could make out nothing but a black shape as he remained there, apparently with his hands in his pockets, softly whistling an unfamiliar tune which seemed to stop short each time, as though the whistler had forgotten or could not manage the last two bars. He had attempted the tune four times when, as though the whistling had been a signal, another man strolled casually up to the house, and handed something to the whistler. The next moment he had gone again, and was lost among the shadowy buildings. The door was shut and the light went out in the hall, but another immediately appeared in an upstair room.

Laura was both puzzled and excited. She was loath to return to her boat now that the house had at last shown signs of life; on the other hand, she felt that Mrs Bradley must be informed of this development. She decided to wait another few minutes to see whether there would be anything else to report, and was well-rewarded. Out of the shadows crept two more men, and after them another man who seemed to wish to follow them without their being aware of him.

The little port was deserted at that time of night, for the shops and the post office had long been shut and the local yacht club was down by the Hard. There was no reason for the hotel residents to roam about after dark, and the hotel bars were not open to the public. Sounds of the ten o'clock news, raucously loud, drowned all other noise except that made by a back-firing automobile in a back street. It was the time for treason, stratagems and spoils, thought Laura, tingling with excitement. Softly she crept after the two men, for the third had melted into the night and she had lost track of him. There was no approach by the front door this time, but a furtive slinking into the shadows at the side of the house. Laura halted and listened. She was anxious to know where the third man was. He made no sign. From the other two she heard first a slight cough, then a faint tinkling.

To anybody of Laura's naturally lawless nature, the sound of broken glass was apt to act as a clarion call to action. She was across the road and in the shadow of the house in no time. A light had been switched on in the downstair room into which she was looking, and, as the curtains had not been drawn together, she could see that the two men who had invaded the house were facing two others. Each man was holding a knife, three men in their right hands, the fourth, who had his back to Laura, in his left. One of the men facing her was the stammering left-luggage clerk who had refused to let her take away Miss Faintley's parcel.

Before the murderous fight began, four words were spoken. The stammerer . . . but he showed no trace of a stammer now . . . . said:

'*Lastrea Filix-Mas!*'

The left-handed man replied, scornfully, '*Asplenium Fontanum!*' Both men spat, and the battle was then joined. The most extraordinary thing about it, in Laura's opinion, was its almost uncanny silence. The room was deeply carpeted so that, except for breathless grunts as the contestants circled round one another, no sound was heard. The room was a large one, running (with folding doors open) from front to back of the house, and, as though it had been prepared as an arena, it was unfurnished except for the carpet.

Laura watched, fascinated. Suddenly the door into the farther room began to open very slowly, and round the opening peered the unlovely visage of Tomson. He also held an open knife.

Now Laura knew nothing much about the other four, and, in any case, they seemed evenly matched; but she had a strong distaste for Tomson. The broken window had been forced open, and the combatants were far too much occupied to notice a silent spectator. She began to scramble over the sill.

'No, you don't!' murmured Bannister's voice behind her. (So *he* had been the third man!) He hauled her back, thrust her roughly aside into some bushes, and leapt into the fray. He tackled Tomson tigerishly. The naked knife shot out of Tomson's hand and slithered along the carpet towards the open window. Laura, who had crawled out of the bushes and was feeling murderous, shot in over the sill and picked up the knife. Then she pulled out the police whistle which Mrs Bradley caused her to carry, and blew and blew and blew.

The electrifying sound acted with its usual magic. Except for Tomson, who was flat out in the middle of the carpet, and Bannister, who stood over him licking his knuckles, the contestants melted away, some by way of the door, the others through the window. One aimed a vicious blow at Laura as he shot past, but she hooked him up neatly, and his head came crashing against the wallpaper.

'But why did you bring the police along so soon?' complained Bannister, when he, Laura and Mrs Bradley were having a night-cap on board *Canto Five* before he returned to his boat to sleep. 'I was just beginning to enjoy myself!'

'That was the reason,' said Laura, squinting into her empty glass. 'I didn't see why you should barge me into the shrubbery and hog all the fun yourself. And where did you come from, anyway?'

'I hadn't gone, you see. I was hanging about to keep an eye on you, because it don't become a young woman to join in private fights.'

'Was Tomson's knife any good?' asked Laura of Mrs Bradley.

'It is hand-made, and closely resembles (so far as my memory serves me) the one with which Miss Faintley was stabbed to death. Detective-Inspector Vardon will no doubt compare them.'

'And are all the gang rounded up?'

'There is no means of telling at present. We took two on board the dredger . . . those who thought to escape by taking out the rusty cruiser . . . and, as you know, five were captured in or near the house. You will probably be asked to identify three of them.'

'Oh, yes. Well, I can swear to the stammering bloke who wouldn't let me have the parcel, but the other two . . . I suppose they're the chaps who removed the case of ferns from Cromlech Down House ... that's going to be more difficult. I'm not hazarding any guesses. If I'm not absolutely positive ... and I don't see how I *can* be ... I ain't saying nothing.'

'Quite right. And now please go and turn in. I want a word with Mr Bannister.'

Laura poured herself another drink.

'Here's to both of you,' she said. 'No heel-taps!' She gulped down the contents of the glass and said rapturously, 'More to-morrow!' Then she removed herself to her bunk, leaving the other two in possession of the saloon.

'It was good of you to answer my call so quickly,' Mrs Bradley said, in tones too low for her secretary to hear.

'I came because of *her*, you know ... Laura.'

'I see. You are aware, I take it, that she is already engaged to be married?'

'She doesn't wear a ring.'

'She dislikes what she calls the badge of servitude. She will probably refuse to wear a wedding-ring, too, when the time comes.'

'Would you mind if I saw her occasionally?'

'I do not think she would make a schoolmaster's wife, but you will be welcome at my house at any time you care to visit us. Good night. I am very glad that you were able to prevent her from making any unmaidenly display of physical prowess. We shall see you in the morning, no doubt.'

But at dawn Bannister put back to Lymington, moored his small boat, and went back to his lodgings by train. Laura, on deck at eight, looked for the yacht, but it was gone.

'Ah, well!' she remarked philosophically to a seagull perched on a bollard. 'What's the matter with a swim?' She untied the dinghy and rowed off, returning with an enormous appetite for breakfast.

CHAPTER FIFTEEN

UNCLE TOM COBLEIGH AND ALL

*

'Now this isn't the end of this shocking affair
. . . and although they be dead, of the horrid career . . . '

'WE ought to have seen a lot sooner that the knife which killed Miss Faintley could be connected with Trench,' said Laura. 'How goes the fernery, young Alice?'

Her friend Alice Boorman, thin, wiry, an athlete and a botanist, looked up from her work of mounting the fifteen specimens of British ferns which Mrs Bradley had asked her to acquire.

'Quite well, I think, Dog. What are they really needed for? Mrs Bradley has already used the ones she wanted. Is this for the jury at the trial? She didn't say, and I didn't like to ask questions she might not want to answer.'

'So you get your information by the back door, do you?' asked Laura, grinning. 'Well, I've no clue to the answer, so it's not a bit of good trying to pump me. She's at Hagford, preparing to convict this gang of smugglers of getting currency out of the country. The ferns, as no doubt you are aware, formed their code.'

'Yes, I know . . . I *think* I know.'

'Cagey, aren't you? But if you will kindly distinguish one from another for me . . . for I confess that my eye for ferns is not as acute as I could wish . . . I will endeavour to reconstruct for you her theory.'

'All right. I say, it was very ingenious, you know.'

'It was. You wait and see. Go on.'

'Well, this is *Blechnum Spicant,* and this is *Lastreas Nephrodium.* Mrs Bradley said I was to mount them almost touching

one another. That means they've got to be taken together,
I suppose.'

'It does, and it's the cleverest of the whole lot, in my
opinion. You see, the code-ferns were sent in two packings,
a flat one made of wood and a small plaster thing in the
form of a statue. The statues were made in France; the
wood came from Kindleford School. The ferns packed in
wood were orders, we think, indicating where the stuff was
to be picked up next . . . for the gang didn't risk shipping
it always from the same place.'

'Well, what about these two ferns? One, in English, is
the Hard Fern, and the other the Buckler Fern, so-called
from its supposed resemblance to a kidney-shaped Roman
shield.'

'There you are, you see. You've said it . . . Buckler's
Hard, on the Beaulieu River.'

'Good gracious! That's clever! Now let *me* do one.'

'Simple when you've got the hang of it, isn't it?'

'Here's *Polypodium Phegopteris*, and here's *Osmunda Regalis*
. . . that's the Beech Fern and the Royal Fern. No, I can't
do it, after all.'

'Mrs Croc. thinks you have to spell the beech with an
A instead of double E.'

'But where was the beach?'

'Go to your next fern.'

'Royal Fern. Well, the only royal place that has a beach
is London, and the beach is near Tower Bridge.'

'There you are, then. That's the way it worked. Of course,
its scope was very limited. You couldn't say much with only
fifteen ferns altogether, especially as some had to be com-
bined, and as there had to be two kinds of packing.'

'Yes, why two kinds? Does Mrs Bradley know?'

'The statues were warnings, she thinks. Can you think of
a cautionary fern?'

Alice pondered over the exhibits, then smiled and picked
out *Asplenium Ceterach*.

'Good. The Scaly Spleenwort,' said Laura. 'Scaly . . .
fairly old-fashioned slang for something not much cared

about. Remember? Now see if you can find the "All Clear" Fern which, we think, had to follow the Scaly Spleenwort to indicate that the lads could go ahead again.'

Alice chose *Asplenium Fontanum*.

'Go to the top of the class,' said Laura heartily. 'Your deductions are the same exactly as those of our revered employer. The Smooth-Rock Spleenwort it is.' She looked narrowly at her friend. 'Seems to me you've been told this before.'

'It's all very well to pick them out when you've been given the clue,' said Alice, ignoring the implied question, 'but it would take a genius like Mrs Bradley to sort it all out in the first place. Well, now, that's done! I had better be off. My leave of absence from school is up, and to-morrow I'm taking a party of girls to see the English Women against Scotland at Wembley. But, one thing. You say these people have been smuggling currency out of the country. What for?'

'Black Market pound notes on the Riviera and so forth, duck. Unpatriotic lads and lasses who find the spending money inadequate can contact these blighters over there and get what currency they like. It's been done before, but never on a scale like this. The willing spenders on holiday have to pay through the nose, of course, and they lay themselves open to blackmail and all sorts of unpleasant consequences, it appears, and serve them right! Stinkers one and all, if you canvass my opinion.'

'What did you mean about Trench and the knife?' asked Alice.

'She meant,' said Mrs Bradley, coming into the room, 'that it was obvious that one could connect secret metalwork as well as secret woodwork with Mr Trench's school centre. His fingerprints,' she added, addressing Laura, 'were on the knife with which Miss Faintley was killed. So much has already been established.'

'So that settles that! Did anything else come out?'

'He pleads Not Guilty, and reserves his defence.'

'He'll never get away with it, will he?'

'I hardly think so. He says that he made the knife for himself as an exercise in metalwork. He does not know, of course, that Tomson's precisely similar knife, thanks to Mr Bannister and yourself, has been impounded by the police. He will find a duplicate knife very difficult to explain, and when it comes to a plethora of similar knives . . . for every gangster had one –'

'Why was that?'

'The knives also served the purpose of a password.'

'Oh . . . like Masonic greetings. One more thing puzzles me. Why a dredger? Clumsy sort of idea, I should have thought!'

'The very last type of ship likely to attract suspicion, child. Nobody in their senses would think of searching a dredger for thousands of English pound notes. The exchange to the rusty cruiser was made very secretly, and the money run into France, probably at some small Riviera port and possibly even with the connivance of some member of the port authority. Owing to a fortunate remark made by Mr Bannister, the French police have found thousands of the pound notes stored in a cave near Lascaux. By the way, you remember refuting my suggestion that I should take a hand in the game and send a fern to Hagford Junction?'

'Don't tell me that you went against my considered judgement and sent a fern after all? Which one did you decide on?'

'*Botrychium Lunaria,* child.'

Alice laughed.

'The Moonwort,' she said. She spoke proudly. 'Mrs Bradley asked my advice, and that was *my* idea.'

'Loony,' said Laura, regarding her friend with sorrowful interest.

'Fortunately, the leader of the gang made the same almost literal translation,' said Mrs Bradley. 'It was then that *Athyrium Filix-Foemina* came into the picture.'

'You didn't send that, too!'

'The Lady Fern, yes, I did . . . at least, I handed it to Trench, poor man. No wonder he tried to kill me with his chisel. He knew it was the writing on the wall, although I don't know that he recognized the fern. Any fern would have done, but I preferred to hand him our signatures.'

'Well, I'm dashed!' said Laura. She spoke respectfully. 'Did you get any more out of Miss Franks about that four hundred pounds?'

'No, but I tackled Miss Faintley's aunt, and pushed her hard. I never believed she was as innocent as she pretended to be. She *must* have known that her niece had another source of income besides the one she earned at school. I challenged her very strongly and gave her a hint as to the extent of my knowledge. As I hoped and expected, she broke down and confessed that as soon as she discovered (or, rather, guessed, I fancy), that Lily Faintley was "up to something", as she expressed it, she was quite determined to obtain some of the pickings for herself.'

'What? She blackmailed her own niece, do you mean?' asked Laura, incredulously. Mrs Bradley cackled.

'It would not be the first time such a thing had been known in families,' she replied. 'And there was no love lost between them, you remember. That fact came out at once, the first time we encountered the older Miss Faintley. She was peevish that her niece had been killed, but neither grief-stricken nor horrified.'

'Yes, that stuck out a mile, as you say. In other words, someone had killed the goose that laid the golden eggs! And did she really try to get four hundred pounds out of niece Lily?'

'Five hundred, to be precise. Lily gave her a hundred, but tried to raise the rest elsewhere. When she did not succeed, she, according to the aunt, "turned nasty" and threatened to put Tomson on the aunt's track, indicating that he was an ally of hers, a prize villain into the bargain, and one who would stick at nothing for the sake of very much less money than the aunt was trying to extort.'

'What a lovely pair!'

'Yes, indeed. The relationship of aunt to niece is often a strange one, however. Miss Faintley, finding that the threat of Tomson had taken effect, then agreed to give her aunt a small proportion of the takings in return for silence and discretion.'

'But you don't think the aunt knew what it was all about?'

'I am pretty sure she did not. I don't think *our* Miss Faintley knew, either, the *extent* of the gang's activities.'

'I wonder how she got into the game? I mean, it isn't the sort of thing you connect with teachers.'

'The truth about that is simple, I imagine. You remember Mark telling us that Miss Faintley wore the badge of a ski-ing club? I think that she ran into the gang abroad when her currency had run out, got herself involved with them and was blackmailed into taking on the job of collecting the parcels. She must have been an ideal choice from their point of view – a teacher at a thoroughly respectable school, and resident so near to Hagford Junction. Trench, of course, with his woodwork and metalwork centre and his continual need of money, was equally valuable to them. More than this I doubt whether we shall ever know, unless some of the gang turn Queen's Evidence, and very likely they will.'

'*Polypodium Vulgare,*' said Laura.

'*Ophioglossum Vulgatum,*' said Mrs Bradley.